"IN JAMES TADD ADCOX'S FIRST NOVEL, *DOES NOT LOVE*, MARITAL LOVE DISINTEGRATES FOR COMPLEX TIME-TESTED REASONS—BUT THIS REELING COUPLE IS PACKAGED IN A GRITTY CONTEMPORARY MILIEU WITH PHARMACEUTICAL HUMAN GUINEA PIGS RUN AMOK UNDERGROUND, AND AN FBI AGENT BOTH CREATING AND PARTICIPATING IN S&M SEX TAPES WITH A LIBRARIAN STAGGERING IN GRIEF OVER HER NUMEROUS MISCARRIAGES. A SWIRL OF CULTURAL SATIRE AND PALPABLE PATHOS."

—CRIS MAZZA, AUTHOR OF *VARIOUS MEN WHO KNEW US AS GIRLS* AND *IS IT SEXUAL HARASSMENT YET?*

"THIS IS A BRISK AND BITING NOVEL, ITS HORRORS ROILING BENEATH A PHARMACEUTICAL TONE. ADCOX DEFTLY SITUATES MARITAL TURMOIL WITHIN THE CONTEXT OF CULTURAL TURMOIL, MAKING *DOES NOT LOVE* A DOMESTIC NOVEL FOR OUR TIMES."

—CHRISTOPHER BACHELDER,

AUTHOR OF *U.S.!*

"NOT SINCE DON DELILLO'S WHITE NOISE HAS A NOVEL MADE ME FEEL AS THOUGH THE EARTH'S AXIS HAS TILTED A HAIR THE WRONG WAY. THIS NOVEL IS BOTH DEADPAN FUNNY AND SINISTER, WRITTEN IN PROSE THAT'S COOL AND CRISP: A SMART PAGE-TURNER. IT'S AS THOUGH REVOLUTIONARY ROAD HAD BEEN WRITTEN BY DENIS JOHNSON, AND THEN SOME MENACING FBI AGENTS WERE THROWN IN. THREE WORDS OF ADVICE: READ THIS BOOK."

—JOHN MCNALLY, AUTHOR OF AFTER THE WORKSHOP

A NOVEL

DOES NOT LOVE

JAMES TADD ADCOX

CURBSIDE SPLENDOR PUBLISHING

Published by Curbside Splendor Publishing, Inc. , Chicago, Illinois in 2014.

First Edition

Library of Congress Control Number: 2014948798

ISBN 978-1-940430-23-2
Edited by Jacob S. Knabb
Designed by Alban Fischer

Manufactured in the United States of America.

www.curbsidesplendor.com

DOES NOT LOVE

I

DOES
NOT
LOVE

VIOLA IS SITTING on the examination table at the doctor's office in a green dress with an empire waist and sky-blue shoes. She is thinking about floating up through the ceiling of the doctor's office. She is thinking about passing through the clouds then coming to the edge of the earth's atmosphere and then continuing onward, past the rim of debris caught in the earth's gravitational pull, past the meteors and the asteroids and so forth, she's not picturing the details too clearly now, past the moon and the earth-like planets, past the unearth-like planets, out of the solar system. Her husband Robert is holding her hand. This is their third miscarriage. Robert is wearing wrinkle-free gray slacks and a wrinkle-free white shirt. The doctor is telling them about how it is possible to have a healthy child even after multiple miscarriages.

"Spontaneously abort," is the term for what Viola's body does and has done with the pregnancies. There is not always a good explanation for it, the doctor explains.

They are cursed, Viola thinks, Viola and Robert and the doctor, to repeat this scene over and over, like ghosts replaying the circumstances of their untimely deaths.

Viola and Robert have a fight in the parking lot of the doctor's office, except that it's not a fight, because Robert is being too reasonable. That's how Robert gets when he's upset: too reasonable. "It would make me feel a hell of a lot better if just for once you'd raise your voice," Viola says.

"I'm not going to raise my voice," says Robert.

Viola wants to go back inside and tell the doctor to get the damn thing out of her. "Then we should go back inside and talk with the doctor," Robert says. "We should discuss our options."

"It doesn't make any sense to have the doctor get it out of me," Viola says. "It's an unnecessary procedure and potentially damaging to my health."

"That's true," Robert says. "I mean that may be true. The part about it being potentially damaging to your—"

"I don't have diabetes," Viola says. "I don't have heart disease, or kidney disease, or high blood pressure or lupus. My uterus contains neither too much nor too little amniotic acid. I don't have an imbalance of my progesterone nor a so-called incompetent cervix. I have had ultrasounds and sonograms and hysteroscopys and hysterosalpingographys and pelvic exams. I have eaten healthy. I have exercised. I have refrained from tobacco and alcohol and caffeine. I have taken folic acid and aspirin and—" Viola starts crying, standing there in the parking lot.

"You've done everything exactly right," Robert says.

"I *know* that," Viola says. "That is what I am trying to *tell* you."

During the drive home, news helicopters fly overhead. On the radio there's a story about another shooting downtown. Outside their windows, rough parts of Indianapolis stream by.

ON THE MIDDAY NEWS the governor of the state of Indiana discusses the downtown shootings. “We will not stand for them,” the governor says. “These shootings. They will not be stood for.”

“Is it true that all of the victims have been associated with the pharmaceutical industry?” asks a reporter.

“I didn’t say it was time for questions,” says the governor.

“Is it true that the shooter was dressed in what appeared to be a fake fur coat and black goggles, brandishing two silver pistols that glowed in the moonlight?”

“No questions,” the governor says.

The governor and his retinue fold themselves back into the governor-van, and they remove themselves from the press conference.

“Was that ‘no questions’ or ‘no question’?” the anchor asks, from his desk at the studio.

“I believe it was the former, Bill.”

The wind picks up throughout the city, a great whistling through trees and between buildings.

VIOLA'S AUNT AND UNCLE arrive from North Carolina. They are prepared to do whatever they can to help. What is there to do? Viola presses her face into her aunt's bony shoulder. Viola's huge uncle walks around the house, testing the structural integrity of the walls. Robert returns from the grocery store.

"I bought a baked chicken," Robert says. "It's . . . I don't know. Normally I would cook something but . . . " Robert removes the baked chicken from its plastic container and puts it on a serving dish, which he places on the carved walnut dining table. He adjusts it. "There," he says.

Viola's aunt and uncle encourage her to eat. "Eat, baby, eat," they say, rubbing her back, stroking her hair. Viola looks down at the baked chicken.

Viola's uncle asks Robert what he thinks about

the secret law. “I’m in favor of it,” Viola’s uncle explains. “I might not be in favor of it under other circumstances, but these are difficult times.”

“Is it about to come back up for a vote?” Robert asks.

“It is unclear whether the secret law requires a vote, constitutionally speaking. Or whether the secret law can be said to be governed by the constitution at all. There is, perhaps, a secret constitution, corresponding to the secret law. One might go so far as to suppose the secret law’s existence to create a secret constitution, through the rules of logical implication. Though I’d expect you know more about that than me . . . ”

“I don’t work in secret law,” Robert says. “I do corporate litigation.”

“How is the corporate litigation world these days?”

“Complicated.”

Viola stays in bed for an entire day. She looks at the blinds. I’ve never liked these blinds, she thinks. Bamboo. They don’t go with anything else. Why do we have these damn blinds.

VIOLA AND HER AUNT get drinks at a country-western themed bar in a strip mall near the actual mall. There are cactus-shaped strings of lights hung from the ceiling and the servers are dressed in cowboy boots and western-wear shirts with name tags on them. Stuffed vultures perch atop plastic tombstones lining the wall.

Viola still looks pregnant. The blond waitress who comes to their table stares at her belly, dubious. According to the doctor, Viola's body should expel the child naturally in several weeks. "I don't want to *expel the child naturally*," Viola says, slightly drunk. "I want it *out of me*."

Several nearby patrons glance over. "My womb is become a grave," drunk Viola says, trying to be quieter.

"What?" says her aunt.

"*My womb is become a grave.*"

Viola's aunt, who never had kids of her own, helps Viola into the car.

"My womb is become a grave," Viola, still a little drunk, whispers to Robert in bed that night.

"Stop it," Robert says. "Your womb is become no such thing."

The next day Viola heroically cleans the bathroom.

Every night for a week after that Viola dreams about giving birth to her dead child. Or, it appears dead, at first, but after a moment it coughs, rubs its eyes, and crawls from the doctor's hands up onto her belly.

"I thought you were dead," Viola says.

"Oh sure," says her son. "I *was*. But according to the ancient laws of pregnancy, after three times, *something* is born. You can't expect to give birth three times without *something* being born."

"I suppose not," Viola says. Sometimes, in the dream, she's back in North Carolina, on the coast, where she lived as a girl with her aunt and uncle, and everything around her has once more been flattened by Hurricane Diana. Other times she's walking through downtown Indianapolis late at night when the first contractions hit, and she gives birth surrounded by empty corporate towers and closed restaurants, terrified that some-

thing or someone will swoop down on her and steal her child before it has the chance to speak.

THE CHIEF OF POLICE says, "This is my good friend John T. Rockefeller, from the FBI. He's here to tell us what the FBI is going to do."

A clean-cut man in a dark suit approaches the microphone. He smiles at the representatives of the media, then assumes a serious expression. "Primarily, the FBI is going to investigate. That's something that the FBI is very good about. The FBI has labs like you wouldn't believe, full of technologies so new they don't even have names yet, and we bring the full weight of this technology to bear on investigating. Plus, the FBI can fit into very tight spaces. Any space large enough for the FBI to get its head into, it can fit into that space. You might think that you have hidden something very well—someplace that you feel no one in a hundred years would think to look—underneath a floorboard, or sewn into the bottom of your mattress, or inside a crack in the wall of your house leading, so far as you know, only to the terrifying emptiness beyond. *In all likelihood, the FBI has already found it.* The FBI will squirm into those spaces you thought forever hidden, and we will find what you have put there. And then we will test those things, in our labs.

"Of course we welcome and even expect the good-faith efforts of local and state police to assist us in these endeavors, keeping always in mind that, no matter how crude their efforts may appear in comparison, we think of them nonetheless as our 'brothers in enforcement' and fellow upholders of the Law . . . "

"I WANT TO BE KIND towards you," Viola says to Robert. Robert is cutting up a tomato for a tomato sandwich. "Ultimately this is your loss, as well as mine. But I'm not sure if I have enough kindness right now to show towards both of us."

"I get that," Robert says. "That makes sense."

"In the future I will probably be kinder," Viola says.

Robert and Viola eat the honestly somewhat disappointing tomato sandwiches that Robert fixed. The tomatoes were beautiful, but not delicious. Later, they drive to a home furnishings store. They wander through aisles full of pepper grinders and salt grinders and ironing boards and extra-thick "European-style" towels. Viola keeps wanting to buy things that don't go with anything else in the house. "Where would we put that?" Robert says.

“I don’t know, Robert, I don’t know. What difference does it make?”

Robert doesn’t have an answer for this.

Inevitably they buy something. Viola holds the pillow that doesn’t go with anything else in the house in her lap on the drive back, and she imagines herself slowly, over the course of months or years, replacing everything in the house with something else, even the floorboards, even the walls.

AT WORK Robert empties documents from storage boxes, puts different-colored sticky notes on each document to identify what role it is to play in the upcoming deposition, then puts each document back in the storage box from which it came. There are mountains of storage boxes. New storage boxes keep arriving, smiling legal clerks rolling them in on handtrucks.

Robert is an associate at an old and prestigious law firm in Indianapolis that has as its clients several energy companies as well as Obadiah Birch Pharmaceuticals, headquartered downtown. Birch has been accused of marketing an erectile dysfunction drug for use in the treatment of Attention-Deficit Hyperactivity Disorder, an unapproved indication and one for which the drug seems wholly unsuited besides. Robert, with his sticky notes and his boxes and boxes of documents, is on the team handling the defense litigation. The lawsuit comes in the wake of several highly-publicized reports of once-rowdy students engaging in uncontrollable, albeit sedate, frottage in middle-school classrooms across the country. Robert doubts the case will go anywhere. Most likely, no one but he and his legal clerks will see a single one of his sticky-noted documents.

The building that houses the firm was designed by the architectural team of Vonnegut & Bohn, whose other work in Indianapolis includes the Ayres Building, the William H. Block Co. Building, and the German Renaissance Revival-style Athenaeum, also known as Das Deutsche Haus. Several of the original Vonnegut & Bohn buildings have been torn down, which is unfortunate, culturally speaking, but many of those that remain are on the register of national historic places.

Bernard Vonnegut, Sr. , of Vonnegut & Bohn, was the grandfather of the writer Kurt Vonnegut, whose name is carved, along with those of Shakespeare, Plato, and Dostoevsky, in a frieze that runs along the outside of the library where Robert's wife Viola works.

"The question from a legal perspective is whether the company specifically encouraged this off-label use," says one of the bright-eyed, smooth-skinned legal clerks.

"Yes," says Robert.

"Of course doctors are free to prescribe off-label uses, if they want to," says the legal clerk. "That's not the issue."

"Right," says Robert, sorting through the delivery that he has ordered for his legal team. "Do you want a corned beef? What do you want?"

"I believe actually I ordered the pastrami."

Robert thinks about the summer between his L1 year and his L2 year, before he met Viola, when he had briefly dated a blond, skinny legal clerk at the firm where he was interning in New York. She had such a good face. It was a long face, but Robert liked it. He keeps up with her occasionally; there is the occasional email. He knows basically nothing about her personal life, but professionally, she is doing quite fine.

I showed a high degree of promise in law school, Robert thinks. I edited my school's law review. I had offers from several more prestigious firms in New York, but chose instead to come here, back to Indianapolis. It was not Viola's first choice, but she understood how important it was to me, the idea of home. She found a job here and for a while it seemed like everything was exactly right.

During breaks he looks up vacation destinations on the internet: Maui, Barcelona, the Black Forest, Tibet. He looks at pictures of foreign destinations and feels a longing.

Robert has so much money but it never feels like that much money.

"How old are you now, Robert?" asks one of the firm's senior partners. "Forty?"

"Thirty-six."

"Thirty-six. That's still quite young. In the grand scheme of things, Robert, that's quite young indeed. You have your whole life ahead of you, Robert."

"Thank you, sir."

"And you have a beautiful wife. Is this your wife?" the partner asks, picking up the framed picture of Viola from Robert's desk.

"Yes sir."

"Beautiful," the senior partner says.

VIOLA'S BODY *naturally expels* the pregnancy. The doctor hands the strange blue child to Viola without asking if Viola wants to hold it. She cradles the strange blue child. She puts two fingers over its closed transparent eyelids. "I'm not very good at mourning," Viola says to the strange blue child. "I'm not sure how to mourn you. I've had dreams about you, but it wasn't like this." Robert stands beside her in the scrubs the hospital has given him. He can't figure out what to do with his hands, whether he should be touching the strange blue child, what. "Robert, it's okay," Viola says. "You can cry too. No one is going to feel strange about it. You're allowed."

They pass the strange blue child around the room. Everyone kisses it, gently, on the forehead.

"I thought this one was going to make it," Viola's uncle tells Robert, in the hallway afterwards. "We bought all these baby toys. We were pretty sure this time. Like we had this feeling, she seemed to be doing so well. And then when we had to take all those toys and things back . . . "

Robert's mother and father, who live in Geist, a suburb north of Indianapolis, arrive at the hospital bearing beautiful boxes of expensive Chinese takeout.

THEY GIVE THE CHILD a name. There is a small ceremony.

ROBERT AND VIOLA go to the new grocery store that has just opened in Indianapolis. It is a wonderful grocery store, two stories, with a rooftop parking deck. They pick up kale and nori and a pair of grassfed steaks. "It's a little too far to come regularly," Robert says. There are beers in the cold beer aisle that Robert has read about on craft brewing blogs: ninety-minute IPAs, one-hundred-and-twenty-minute IPAs. Next to the refrigeration unit is a table set up for a beer tasting. A tall black man wearing a serious expression hands Robert a small plastic cup of beer. "It's infused with basil," he says. "I think it actually tastes quite remarkable."

Viola and Robert sit at the coffee and wine bar at the front of the new grocery store, drinking coffee and flipping through a copy of *NUVO*, the free weekly. There's an arts festival at Eagle Creek Park.

"Those are always horrible," Viola says. "Some

band playing like covers of Steppenwolf and a bunch of booths selling pictures of trees."

Robert gives her a look. "I don't mean it wouldn't be fun," Viola says. "It might be fun. We can go, if you want."

They get lost, momentarily, in the vast expanses of parking lot, but soon orient themselves, and find their car.

"I'm pretty sure it's a sign," Viola says.

"What is?" says Robert.

Viola makes a gesture in the air that means, You know. "We both know I'd be a terrible mother," she says. "This is like God saying, Viola, honey, you and I both know you'd let the poor thing drown in a bathtub."

"I don't think that's funny," Robert says.

"Neither do I," says Viola.

That night they sit on their back porch and Robert drinks a glass of the quite remarkable basil-infused beer. "It's kind of wheaty," Robert says. "In addition to the basil." The night is so clear through the trees.

"Do you remember how things were when we first moved here together?" Viola asks. "When we were first married?"

"In what sense?"

"In a general sense."

"I think so."

Viola stands and walks off towards the little wood on the edge of their property. She stands between the trees, and turns to face Robert. Moonlight illuminates her face. "The laws of physics work equally well in both directions; what we interpret as entropy is, perhaps, only our preference for one state of matter over another. When you and I were first married, there was a great sense of possibility in the world. We were in love with this possibility, as much as we were in love with each other. Which is to say: we did not know what was to come. Perhaps we still would have married each other, if we knew what was to come. Perhaps we would have married each other in any case. Contemporary science teaches us that all moments in time exist simultaneously. It is imaginable that some other beings, beings greater than us, could look across points in time the way we look across points in space. For such a being, the idea of loss would be unimaginable. For us, however . . . " Viola gestures, as if trying to capture something with her hand that she could not quite fit into words. After a moment she walks back, and resumes her seat on the porch.

That night Viola sleeps fitfully. Robert keeps having to wake her up to get her to stop flinging her limbs all over the place.

VIOLA'S AUNT AND UNCLE wave goodbye from the security gates of the newly remodeled Indianapolis airport, while Viola clutches a wad of tissues in her fist.

At home that night, Robert makes linguine with peanut sauce, using three tablespoons minced fresh garlic, a half tablespoon ground ginger, one half cup honey, a quarter cup soy sauce, three tablespoons rice vinegar, a quarter cup peanut butter, and a good helping of chili powder to make the sauce.

On television a man is saying, "That's what I really like about this city, if you have an idea, you can just go out and do it. This is a city that is always looking for the next new thing."

Later, in bed, Viola pushes Robert away. "I don't want to be touched right now. It's okay for you to be nearby. But I don't want to have someone else actually touch me right now." What she cannot explain is the way it is overwhelming, how his touch is connected to the thing she is feeling right now. Robert of course cannot help feeling hurt.

"It will be better later Robert."

Robert is quiet. Viola can feel the hurt radiating off of him like heat.

VIOLA RETURNS to the ancient neighborhood public library where she works. Now a young FBI agent is there. No one seems to talk about him. He is a sudden, accepted fact, as indisputable as the shelves or the wheezing computers. Every once in a while he catches Viola or one of the other librarians on their breaks, and tries to talk to them about the secret law.

"I feel like we haven't done a particularly good job of clarifying our position, with regard to libraries and the secret law," he says, "and if there's anything that the Bureau hates, it's needless animosity based on simple misunderstandings." He is very charming. Yearning, Viola thinks. There's something about him that yearns.

Of course there have been news stories about FBI agents in libraries around the country. But it seems weird, she thinks, for there to be one specifically in my library, which after all is not even the main library branch in Indianapolis.

Viola tells Robert about the FBI agent that evening. "He's a slick fucking fascist," she says. "Very personable. A fascist for the new millennium."

"Fight the power," Robert says.

"Robert I'm serious."

Robert looks up from his work. Robert is a "fiscal conservative."

Viola feels as if she has been handed a mission, now that the FBI agent is there. There are once more things in the world to do. She prints up a set of quarter-page fliers that say, "Do you know what your child is reading? The FBI might." She begins distributing these to patrons. Because she's a children's librarian, and nearly anything in the vicinity of her desk immediately becomes covered in crayon, before long every one of the fliers she had printed up is decorated with a smiley face, flower, or shaky but recognizable dog, all of which, Viola feels, somewhat dampens her message.

The branch manager asks if he can speak with Viola in his office. "Are you okay?" he says.

"Yes. I'm fine. Thank you for your concern."

"You can take more time off if you need to."

"I'm fine."

"You can't just be fine," Viola's friend Elizabeth

says, later, in the break room. They are waiting for the coffee machine to finish brewing. Like the library that surrounds it, it is an ancient coffee machine, without automatic shutoff, and takes forever to brew.

"Yes, I can. I'm over it," Viola says. "I decided."

"Aren't there stages?"

"Stages have been discredited by the most recent theoretical models," Viola says. "The most recent theoretical models tend to view over-it-ness as a negotiation, by and large."

Viola pictures herself saying the meanest thing she can think of to Elizabeth, for no reason. She pictures Elizabeth crying and asking her, Viola, why she would say such a thing. Viola would shrug and say, No reason.

You are completely unloved, Viola would say. Even your father who lives with you and your two dogs view you primarily as a convenience.

The FBI agent finds Viola while she's smoking a cigarette by the dumpsters behind the library. Viola quickly stubs out the cigarette.

"I don't really smoke," she says, feeling suddenly guilty, for no good reason she can think of.

"You know, I actually really admire what you're doing," the FBI agent says, taking a packet of cigarettes from his inside jacket pocket. He's olive-skinned and black-haired, with lips that pout like an Italian model's. He's a couple of years younger than her, at least. "Though we are approaching it from opposite directions, both of us, I feel, are acting out of love for the principles of freedom."

"What are you doing here?" Viola asks. "This isn't even the main branch in Indianapolis."

"I am a messenger of the secret law," the FBI agent says. "The secret law operates on the periphery every bit as much as the center. The secret law, in fact, recognizes no such center. The secret law is infinite, stretching in all directions." He squeezes off the glowing tip of his cigarette between his thumb and forefinger, puts the ash out with the sole of his gleaming black shoe before heading back inside.

Across the street from the ancient neighborhood library, a gang of African-American bikers hang out in the parking lot of a liquor store, attempting to stare down a group of young hoodlums who have begun to hang out in the empty lot next to the liquor store. Occasionally one of the bikers revs his motorcycle, as if in warning. The bikers sometimes come into the library to use the bathroom, because there's no bathroom in the liquor store. They are always faultlessly polite when they do.

"Is Dude your new boyfriend?" one of the bikers asks Viola.

"Who?"

"That dude who was just out here. Keeps giving you those looks."

"No, I'm married," Viola says.

"Well anyway I'd watch out for him. That dude has some bad mojo."

"Ricky's always concerned about the mojo of things," says one of the other bikers.

"You can tell a lot about a person by their mojo," says Ricky, sounding defensive.

"The fascist told me that he admired me," Viola says to Robert, that night. "Can you fucking believe that? Like maybe I'd swoon because some fascist tool told me that he admired my principles?"

"Are you doing okay?" Robert asks.

"I'm sad, of course," Viola says. "I'm allowed to be sad."

"Well sure. Of course. I'm sad too."

Viola has an image of the two of them, her and Robert, clinging together, moving from room to room like that, making sandwiches, washing dishes, etcetera. "But I feel like the thing to be done's get back to life as normal," she says.

VIOLA PUSHES ROBERT down onto their bed and straddles him. She is dressed in a blue t-shirt. Robert is still wearing his boxers, tugged down now to just below his cock. He can feel Viola push him inside of her, she is rocking back and forth. There is a moment where neither of them is thinking. Viola slaps Robert, grabs at his arms, slaps him again. Robert pushes her off and stares at her.

"That wasn't working for you?"

"No," Robert says. "You slapped me. I mean—you fucking slapped me."

"It just occurred to me. Like maybe you'd like it."

"No, I don't like it. It fucking hurt."

"I thought maybe you'd slap me back," says Viola, in a small hurt voice that grates more than a little on Robert's nerves.

"We've tried that. You said you wanted me to

hit you, and I tried it, and you said you didn't like it after all."

"You just seemed so. . .uncomfortable, that time. I thought maybe it would come more naturally if I hit you first."

"Well it didn't," says Robert, folding his penis back into his underwear and stalking off to the bathroom. When he returns, Viola has disappeared. He sits on the couch breathing steadily for a while, and then goes to look for her. She's in the upstairs bathroom, with the door locked.

"Viola," says Robert.

"What."

"Viola."

"I'm embarrassed," Viola says, from the other side of the locked bathroom door.

"Look, I'm more than willing to try things," Robert says. "You know that. We've talked about it. But I like to be given a heads-up, that's all. That seems fair, doesn't it?"

"I think I'm going to stay in here for a little while," Viola says. "I'm not mad at you."

She doesn't sound embarrassed, Robert thinks. She sounds upset. Robert can feel himself getting angry again, a rising motion, angrier and angrier.

Robert, as a rule, is not used to being angry. He's used to being level-headed. This thing that has been happening, where he feels like he's put in a situation where he gets angrier and angrier and has nothing whatsoever that he can do about it, is a new situation, one that he is unfamiliar with.

Robert considers the possibilities: He could break down the damn door. Breaking down the damn door could, to a certain manner of thinking, be seen as acting out of concern for his wife.

"I'm considering breaking down the door," Robert says. "I feel like that could be seen as acting out of concern for you. Would you see that as acting out of concern for you?"

"No."

Robert goes to bed, alone. Robert buys new two-hundred-and-fifty-dollar running shoes.

There's a pattern to it, Robert thinks. He is running along 38th street. He passes the Indianapolis Museum of Art and then he is running on the sidewalk that follows the edge of Crown Hill Cemetery, final resting place of Benjamin Harrison, the 23rd president of the United States; "Indiana poet" James Whitcomb Riley; Howard Garns, the inventor of Sudoku; seven vice presidents; and Dr. Richard Jordan Gatling, inventor of the Gatling gun. Also of course infamous criminal John Dillinger, whose grave is nearly impossible to find without a map.

She gets upset, Robert thinks. And it's like I can tell she's about to get upset before she even realizes it's happening, maybe even before I realize it's happening. Muscle-memory, Robert thinks. My organism recognizes the particular signs of her organism getting upset. So much of what we know is purely physical, Robert thinks: we know so much in our bodies before we know it consciously. Well, it makes sense. We've lived together for what, four years now. And then before that knowing each other in Ann Arbor, another year or so. It is an almost Pavlovian response, Robert thinks. She gets upset and it puts me in this defensive crouch, where I am doing everything I can to calm her down, to make her less upset. And then when the situation is over, I get angrier and angrier.

I don't remember her getting upset like this in Ann Arbor, Robert thinks. Not in the same way. Or maybe just not towards me?

Once I was famous for being level-headed among my friends. Conversations about me often mentioned my level-headedness in celebratory terms. But perhaps there is only so much upsetness that the organism can take, aimed at it, like it has a maximum amount that it can absorb before it is full. Full of upsetness.

At the North United Methodist Church he encounters his friend Luis, also outfitted in running gear.

"Didn't know you ran," says Luis.

"Just started back up," says Robert, jogging in place.

"Those are some fancy-looking shoes, Guay."

"Brand new," Robert says. "How is Cynthia?"

"That place on her head is getting bigger. They're still not sure what it is."

"I'm sorry to hear that."

"She's a champ. She keeps her spirits up. How's Viola?"

"Good," Robert says. "Real good."

"I heard you two were expecting?"

"No."

"Are you sure?"

"Pretty sure."

They part ways and Robert heads north on Meridian. Robert repeats the word "expecting" over and over in his head, until it loses all meaning and becomes a sort of melody, keeping time with his footfalls: ex-pec-*ting*, ex-pec-*ting*, ex-pec-*ting*. The blighted storefronts near 38th give way to tree-lined streets and large, beautiful houses set far back from the road.

"HAVE YOU THOUGHT about getting something?" Robert asks Viola. He's still sweating from his run. He thinks about toxins, sweating them out. Do you sweat toxins out? Is that a real thing?

"Getting something?" Viola asks. She's sitting at the kitchen table, reading. There's a light breeze from the open kitchen window.

"Like to help you through this."

"I feel really resistant to the idea of drugs, Robert. I've talked about it with my talk therapist."

"What does she say?"

"She says that drugs can occasionally be helpful in situations like mine, but that the choice is ultimately up to me."

"Well sure. Obviously."

"This is grief, Robert. It's a process."

Robert takes a shower in the master bathroom upstairs, and looks for fresh clothes. They need to do laundry. There is no underwear left in his best underwear drawer, so he gets out a pair from his second-best underwear drawer. He sits on the bed in the master bedroom, thinking. Later, he returns to the kitchen, where Viola is emptying the dishwasher.

"That was probably not the best way to respond, the other night," he says. "Getting angry the way I did. I'm sorry about that. It's just that we hadn't, I mean . . . "

"What?" says Viola, placing a newly clean serving bowl on the counter.

"Like there was a while where you didn't even want me to touch you. That felt horrible. And then, a couple of nights ago, I guess it came as a surprise."

"Oh Robert," Viola says.

Viola pushes back Robert's still damp hair from his forehead. She thinks: This is my husband, for whom I care very much. She thinks at the same time: I could live without him.

The ways emotions are layered, Viola thinks, and how you often can't tell which one is the real one and which one is the one you are playing at.

ROBERT AND VIOLA go to a park near their house and wander around underneath the trees. The weather is suddenly beautiful. In the park Viola and Robert spend a long time watching a squirrel attempt to carry a plastic bag up a tree. "Maybe it's stuck to him somehow?" Viola says. "Like, maybe he was eating something inside the bag and it got caught?" The squirrel keeps getting its legs tangled in the plastic bag. Viola feels a rising sense of panic. "Maybe we should help?" she says.

"How would we help?" asks Robert.

"I'm just afraid he's going to fall," says Viola, her voice suddenly too high.

That night she looks through websites about potential surrogate mothers. There's no reason to assume that the problem is on my end, she thinks. But I do. Why do I just assume that? If after all they don't know why the miscarriages are occurring . . .

For each of the surrogate mothers there's information about her ethnic background, her education, her interests, whether she speaks any languages in addition to English, etcetera. In some cases, there is a short personal statement.

"I believe that the gift of life is the most important thing one human being can give to another. I am a graduate student studying Mathematics with a particular interest in Riemannian geometry. My other interests include hiking and the struggle of the people of Myanmar, formerly known as Burma."

Viola goes into the next room, where Robert is working at his desk. "My interest in them feels prurient," she says.

"In who?"

"The women on these websites. All of their eyes are blacked out, did you know that? With those little black bars. It's for privacy, but it still comes across as dirty, you know?"

Robert follows Viola to the next room and looks at pictures of women on the surrogate mother website, with their eyes blacked out.

"I thought we weren't going to worry about this right now," Robert says.

"I'm not worried about it," Viola says. "I was just looking."

ROBERT AND VIOLA watch a DVD of Akira Kurosawa's *Throne of Blood*. The room around them begins to thicken with ghosts. From the crowd of ghosts, Viola's mother steps forward, her face a mask of white powder, dark lines drawn in kohl around her eyes and mouth.

"What are you looking for?" Viola's ghost-mother asks, impatiently. Viola realizes, abruptly, that she had been scanning the crowd of ghosts.

"I guess," Viola starts, then says, "Nothing. Never mind. It's stupid." Then: "There's that one Gwendolyn Brooks poem? About how she feels the presence of the children she might have had? Not ghosts, exactly, but potential ghosts?"

"A Gwen what poem?"

"Never mind. I already said it was stupid."

"Little baby potential ghosts," Viola's ghost-mother says, taking in the room, which is a much nicer room than any room she'd lived in. She passes her hand through this object and that. "Aren't you precious."

Viola's ghost-mother passes her hand through a side lamp and ends her tour of the room facing Robert. Robert frowns at the screen, seemingly deep in thought. She gives him a long arch look before shaking her head. "This guy?"

"What, Robert? My husband, who you weren't around to meet? He's good," Viola says. "He's stable. Dependable. I know that sounds like faint praise, but it's actually kind of rare, as it turns out."

"Robert," Viola's ghost-mother says, drawling the name out. She makes a face. "Bob. Bobby."

"It's just Robert."

"He's boring," Viola's ghost mother says.

"He's stable. Though I'm not one-hundred percent surprised you don't know the difference. He's been there for me. That's something I figured out that I need."

Viola's ghost-mother passes her hand through the crotch of Robert's pants. "Not terrible," she says, after a moment. "Still, he doesn't get you off."

"Whose sex life is exciting after four years? We've talked about the possibility of an open relationship."

"But he doesn't want that."

"I don't know that *I* want it," Viola says. "I think I'd rather him get some on the side and just not know. He'd be careful. He wouldn't put my health in danger, which is the main thing. I trust him."

"You really think this guy would try to get some on the side?" Viola and her ghost-mother watch Robert watching *Throne of Blood*: the banquet scene, in which the new emperor, driven mad by his murderous acts, is drawing his sword on thin air. "Milquetoast!" Viola's ghost-mother calls at Robert.

"He's been willing to explore things with me."

"Isn't that nice of him?" In the crowd of ghosts, various ghosts pass through the objects in the room, bump into each other, fall down, get up. Other ghosts just stand there, mouths open, silent. "Look, Vivi, we both know there's a difference between 'being willing' and fucking your brains out."

Viola looks down at one of the smaller, clumsier ghosts, who's fallen squat at her feet. "I'd forgotten that you called me that. Did you always call me that?"

"What, Vivi?"

"My aunt calls me that. I thought that was her name for me."

"It's a family name," Viola's ghost-mother says, helping the clumsy ghost right itself. "You had a great-grandmother who lived to something like a hundred and twelve, that's what we used to call her."

Both of them watch the smaller, clumsy ghost wander away, bump into another ghost, fall down near the doorway to the kitchen. Viola gets a little weirdly choked up.

"The fuck do you even *presume*," she says. "I am feeling some very reasonable anger right now. Some abandonment issues. All *very* reasonable. Stemming from for example how I haven't seen you in twenty-five years or so. And when I do? You want to like, criticize my life decisions. Me, being angry right now? Me, raising my voice? Very, very reasonable."

"I know what you thought of me, Vivi."

Viola stands and starts picking things up, books, magazines, old cups, but in her anger isn't sure what to do with them, so she starts putting them back where they were. "You know what? Don't call me Vivi. Don't fucking even."

"You were afraid of me. You didn't want me to come back."

"I was six years old," Viola says. "Jesus. I don't have to defend my six-year-old self to you. Grow up."

Viola's ghost-mother who is actually a year

or two younger than Viola looks at her for a long moment, eyebrows raised. “Right,” Viola says. “I guess that’s not something you can actually do at this point. But still.”

On the television screen the emperor is shot full of arrows. He stumbles, breaking off the ends of the arrows, a look of wild disbelief across his face. More arrows. “Did they do an okay job, your aunt and uncle?” Viola’s ghost-mother says.

“Great,” Viola says. “They did a really fantastically great job.” A coldness spreads throughout her body. She is not looking at her ghost-mother now.

“I’m glad,” Viola’s ghost-mother says. “I was jealous of them, you know that? I gave her hell for marrying that fat-ass, but I was jealous of them. I wish I had something to give you, Vivi, some sort of advice or something like that. I feel like I didn’t really ever give you anything.”

“I was fine,” Viola says, still cold.

Viola’s ghost mother shakes her head sadly, but whether at Viola or herself is unclear.

Mists envelope the image on the television screen. The ghosts slowly make their way from the room, Viola’s ghost-mother among them. There is a single piercing note from a Japanese flute as the last of the ghosts exit.

“Do you want more wine?” Robert asks. “There’s maybe enough for another glass.”

“It’s okay, you go ahead.”

AT THE INDIANAPOLIS MUSEUM OF ART is an exhibition of dozens of tiny rooms set behind glass. Each room is labeled: Louisiana Bedroom, South Carolina Bedroom, Virginian Drawing Room, and so on. Robert and Viola wander through the exhibition, peering through the glass. Displays throughout the exhibition show how craftsmen had built e.g. the tiny chairs, joining the joints the same way one would built a similar life-sized chair. Everything is exactly to scale, one inch to one foot; the rooms are each about two hand lengths high. Something about the tiny rooms makes Robert nervous, or makes him feel like he is out of place, maybe.

"I am working on acceptance. I am thinking about it as a sort of project," Viola says. "My friend Nikola on the internet suggested to me the idea of the pink bubble."

“Pink bubble?” Robert says.

“You imagine putting the thing you find distressing in a pink bubble, and then you picture it floating gently out into the distance. You tell yourself that it will be okay, this thing, it will be safe in the pink bubble, and you let it go. Off into the distance. It’s a meditation technique.”

“Why pink?”

“I don’t know. Other colors might be okay too.”

“Does it work?”

“Sometimes I think it helps.”

Above the fireplace in the Virginia Drawing Room is a mirror that reflects their faces back to them, full-sized among the miniature tables, chairs, vases, rugs. Viola puts her hand to her mouth and leans in to get a better view. For a moment, the effect is quite shocking.

She imagines a craftsman working over a single chair in the Virginia Drawing Room, spending hours or days on it, getting it right, getting it not-quite-right, starting over. At no point do you know that what you are doing is the right thing to do. You could be wasting all of your time, doing the wrong thing.

I am thirty-four years old, Viola thinks. Soon I will be middle-aged, and after that, old.

Through each of the rooms’ windows are

miniature bushes, trees, gardens. The windows have been designed so that one can imagine the scene going on and on into the world outside the windows, so that the viewer can't quite see where it all stops.

"Someone had to make all of this," Robert says suddenly, as if it had just occurred to him. "By hand. Someone had to carve each of the legs of that table. Someone had to carve each of the drawers of that dresser." Robert and Viola look through the glass into the little room, at the miniature dresser. "Do you think they open?" Robert asks.

Robert and Viola examine a framed schematic of the dresser, drawn in pencil.

"They open," Robert says.

At the end of the exhibition, there's a book for sale, containing full-page color photographs of each of the rooms. "They just look like rooms," Robert says, disappointed, as he flips through the book.

Robert and Viola drink ginger-infused ice water in the café at the front of the art museum and look out at the giant windows that cover most of the wall. "It might stop," Viola says. "We have no assurance whatsoever that it won't."

"What might?"

"How from here you can see trees and beyond them, cars, but somewhere beyond all of that, just beyond where you can see, it might just, you know. Stop."

"How are things going with your FBI agent?"

"He's not my FBI agent," Viola says. "I haven't claimed him."

"I have some contacts in the CIA, maybe," Robert says. "Guys I knew from law school."

"I'm not sure how much good a CIA contact would do," Viola says. "I think there's a pretty high degree of animosity between the FBI and the CIA."

"Sure, but with the recent attempts to consolidate the intelligence community . . ."

"How is your case? The case you're working on?"

"Fine. It's fine," Robert says, in the voice that he uses when he doesn't want to talk about something.

Robert and Viola stare out the window, imagining some place beyond what they can see, where the cars and parking lot asphalt and trees and people might suddenly, terrifyingly stop.

"DO YOU WANT TO TRY having sex again?" Viola asks Robert.

"Okay." Viola kneads Robert's erection through his boxers. Robert massages Viola's breast through the t-shirt that she wears to bed. Viola takes Robert's hand and puts it between her legs.

Robert decides to remodel the house.

"The whole house?" Viola asks. "Just like that?"

"No of course not, not the whole house," Robert says. "Something small. I was thinking maybe the downstairs bathroom, just the countertops and the sinks, actually."

Robert pictures the joy of working with his hands. He imagines the satisfaction of starting a job and finishing it and knowing, once he had, that it was finished. At the hardware store, there to examine different kinds of faucets, he finds himself instead wandering off to the lumber aisle and breathing in the smell of untreated wood. The possibilities of newness are overwhelming.

"Black marble," Robert says. "The countertops. Kitchen and bathroom. What do you think about black marble?"

Viola gives it some thought. She is trying to be supportive. "I think it might be a little ostentatious," she says. "I feel like it's something that's very fashionable right now but will very possibly look dated in a few years."

"Ostentatious," Robert says, screwing up his face. Robert scrutinizes the kitchen isle.

"I'm not even sure I wanted a kid," Viola says to her aunt, on the telephone. "Robert, he definitely wanted a kid."

"You'd be a great parent," her aunt says.

"I'd be terrible. I'm pretty sure this is a sign. Like, I'd be watching a movie or just getting to the really good part of a book or something, and that's when the terrible thing would happen. The kid would find the matches or stick something in a socket or drown in the bathtub. This is God saying: Viola, honey, you and I both know that you'd let the poor thing drown in the bathtub."

Viola's aunt laughs, a great hacking laugh.

Viola considers the possibilities of opening a

bottle of wine at ten-thirty a.m. on a Thursday. The arguments against opening the bottle of wine, for the most part, have to do with antiquated cultural norms, Viola thinks.

"Do you believe that life is the most important gift that one human being can give another?" Viola asks her friend Tabitha, who has come over for coffee.

"What else is there?" Tabitha asks.

"We don't generally consider it to be taking something away from someone if we don't give life to someone who was never alive in the first place," Viola says. "Outside of certain fundamentalist religions, there is no commonly recognized onus on people of childbearing age to bear children."

"I think you would be a really good mother," Tabitha says.

"That's not the point."

On television, commercials herald end-of-the-world survival courses: it's a franchise deal, with the local version being taught in a nearly abandoned mall on Lafayette Street. Such courses rose to prominence just before the new millennium, in response to Y2K fears, and have persisted, fed on a steady occurrence of new signs and dates: the fall of the twin towers, the evangelical minister Harold Camping's predictions of the Rapture, the end of the Mayan calendar in 2012. A survivalist, interviewed by a local news station, recommends an "end times emergency kit," consisting of a compass, a canteen, waterproof matches, iodine tablets, a fixed-blade knife with a full tang, a hatchet, a sewing kit, waterproof bags, maps (local and national).

"Condoms actually work quite well as watertight containers for smaller objects," the end-times survivalist says. "It's worth keeping in mind that life without electricity and running water and heat is a very different kind of life than what we're used to here in America."

Viola and Tabitha look through the paper at the weekend events. Now they are drinking wine. "What do you think about the shootings downtown?" Tabitha asks.

"I haven't really been paying attention," Viola admits.

"Doesn't Robert work for that pharmaceutical company?"

"He doesn't work for them. He works for a law firm, and they are a client of his firm."

Viola reads: "This discovery (alienation) of conditions takes place through the interruption of happenings. The most primitive example would be a family scene. Suddenly a stranger enters. The mother was just about to seize a bronze bust and hurl it at her daughter; the father was in the act of opening the window in order to call a policeman. At that moment the stranger appears in the doorway. This means that the stranger is confronted with the situation as with a startling picture: troubled faces, an open window, the furniture in disarray. But there are eyes to which even more ordinary scenes of middle-class life look almost equally startling."

Viola folds over the edge of the page and puts the book down on the coffee table and looks at a small statuette, a replica Rodin, sitting under a lamp on a small table beside the bookshelf.

"It's possible that I may not be in love with you anymore," Viola says carefully, lying next to Robert that night. Robert is quiet in a way that makes Viola think that he maybe already knew.

"Do you want to stay married?" he says, finally.

IN THE MORNING, Robert takes stock of their house. It has a large living room connected to an open kitchen, with a kitchen island forming a sort of border between the two. The downstairs contains as well a dining room, a guest bedroom, and a half bath. A set of stairs leads from the living room to an "open"-style second floor, with a wrap-around hallway leading to the bedroom, full bath, and an office that looks out on the street. The walls could use repainting, he thinks. Something darker, more serious. It is true that white walls open a place up, but they scuff so easily. Robert walks around the house, examining scuffs in the off-white walls. It's the default choice, Robert thinks, white walls. There's no particular cause for it. They don't *mean* anything. Robert pictures the walls in new colors: burgundy, beige, a light but stately blue.

AT THE LIBRARY, the FBI agent presents Viola with a National Security Letter. “I am in love with you, desperately,” he says, handing over the order. “Your very resistance to the secret law that I serve has won my heart. You are hereby forbidden as per section 520 of the secret law from discussing any aspect of our interactions, or for that matter so much as acknowledging the existence of said interactions. I will be emailing you with a series of questions, pertinent to an ongoing investigation, that you are to answer precisely and in full. Failure to comply with this order incurs the severest penalties of the secret law, up to and including disappearance.”

“But this is ridiculous,” Viola says, staring down at the order. “People have seen us interacting. Everyone at the library knows that you’re here.”

“The secret law makes no distinction between

the known and the ought-to-be-known. You are to comply with the order exactly as it is written."

Viola goes to get after-work martinis with Elizabeth, from circulation. It's the first time that they've gotten after-work martinis since Viola came back. "Those flowers on your desk," Elizabeth says. "All those roses. Are they from Robert? Is he trying to make up for something?"

"I don't think I'm allowed to say who they're from," Viola says, frowning.

"A secret admirer?" Elizabeth asks, faux-scandalized.

"Do you think that that man outside would give me a cigarette?" Viola says.

The man outside wants to talk to Viola about the dangers of the New World Order. Viola smokes and smiles at Elizabeth, uncomfortably, through the glass. Elizabeth smiles back. "That's what you get for smoking," she says, when Viola returns.

"I THOUGHT our relationship was good," Robert says. He and Viola are sitting on the edge of their bed. Robert is staring down at the carpet. "I thought we were strong. That we were going to be strong together, throughout this difficult time."

"Robert, it is good. In many ways it is very good. Possibly in all of the ways that count." Viola gets undressed. Robert gets undressed. Robert has a patch of sandy blond hair that extends in a nearly straight line from his navel to his pubis.

"Robert, I want you to touch me like you don't care about me. That is what I want from you right now."

"I don't know that I can do that," Robert says.

Viola closes her eyes tightly. "Robert, please. Robert please just please."

At work, Robert thinks about the deposition. The questions that the case raises are important, but they are far off, beyond the horizon. Robert is adrift in a sea of facts, small facts, facts that float meaninglessly through and beyond his life.

VIOLA BUYS an instructional DVD on rough sex. A gratingly cheerful woman demonstrates on a smiling fellow porn-star the body parts that can be safely hit and how, how hard, etcetera. Several famous rough-sex porn stars give testimonials about their experiences. “I think that any man who has never been dominated isn’t really a man,” says one, a youngish balding porn star lounging shirtless on a bed with burgundy sheets. “I can’t watch this,” says Viola, who has become suddenly, painfully embarrassed.

Robert, alone in his office downstairs, watches the instructional DVD on his laptop while Viola is at work. “A lot of times I find it really hot to start gentle and build up to higher intensities,” the cheerful woman says, demonstrating on her likewise cheerful assistant. Robert writes down: Start gentle and build to higher intensities. Robert resumes the DVD and continues watching it, scanning his notes.

Robert and Viola discuss the concept of safewords. "I don't understand why you wouldn't just tell me to stop, if you wanted me to stop," Robert says.

"It's not just for me," Viola says. "You could use the safeword too."

"Why wouldn't I just stop?"

Robert is really not trying to be obtuse. It's that he feels that the whole safeword thing calls their mutual trust into question. Of course he would stop, as soon as he realized that she wanted to stop. Why would they need a special word for that?

Robert holds Viola down on their bed. He slaps her. "I'm sorry," Viola says, shaking her head.

"What?" says Robert, suddenly burning with self-consciousness.

"It doesn't," Viola tries to explain. "I don't know, it just feels awkward." He's trying so hard, she thinks. Which is of course part of the problem.

Her talk therapist seems uncomfortable talking about Viola's sex life. "Do you think these . . . desires . . . may have some connection with the recent losses you've experienced?"

"No," Viola says. "It just didn't seem as important to insist on it before, somehow."

“Hm,” Viola’s talk therapist says, looking carefully away from her.

Robert watches the DVD again in the fading light from his office window. What was awkward, he thinks. What was so fucking awkward.

NEAR THE DUMPSTERS behind the library, Viola talks with Ricky, the African-American biker, about mojo.

"From the West African mojuba," Ricky says, "meaning a prayer or homage; more broadly understood in contemporary Hoodoo as one's overall spiritual valence, akin to for example the Japanese notion of life-force or Ch'i."

"Chee?" says one of the other bikers.

"Nah," says Ricky, "it's pronounced 'key.'"

"Hoodoo," Viola says.

"Well sure, that's where mojo comes from, the Hoodoo system of beliefs."

THE YOUNG HOODLUMS across the street have taken to experimenting with small explosives. So far nothing they've blown up has been of any importance, but it's a concerning development nonetheless.

VIOLA TAKES a late lunch at an Indian place up the street from the library. Sitar versions of popular songs play, piped in from speakers hidden behind silk plants. The restaurant is nearly empty. Viola sits at a table near the back waiting for her chicken masala, reading a young adult novel about a plucky young girl who transforms into a squid to escape the semi-romantic intentions of her evil stepfather. Plucky young girls turning into things are a staple of the sort of young adult novels that Viola reads. Viola reads a lot of young adult novels, because of her job, of course, but she suspects that young adult novels would be most of what she read as an adult in any case.

She never read young adult novels when she was actually a young adult. When she was a young adult, she read the British Romantics.

She's just gotten to the part about the squid-girl's new life underwater when the FBI agent sits down at her table. "Viola St. Clair?"

"Did you follow me here?" Viola says. "Jesus, you followed me here."

"You are magnificent," the FBI agent says. "Can I buy you a drink, Ms. St. Clair?"

Viola starts to say something, pauses, tries again, quieter. "I'm just having lunch. And it's Mrs. Also, Wilder-St. Clair. With, you know, a hyphen."

The waiter, seemingly unbidden, brings two gin-and-tonics.

"Hope you're thirsty," Viola says, pushing hers towards the FBI agent. He pushes it back. Viola takes a little sip, just because she's feeling so damn *awkward*, really.

"Cigarette?" the FBI agent says, producing a pack.

"There's no smoking in here. Besides, I'm not really a smoker."

"I know the owner. We have an understanding."

The FBI agent lights Viola's cigarette. A waiter rushes to their table carrying an ornate ashtray featuring painted scenes from the history of the Gupta empire, so delicate that Viola feels a twinge of guilt each time she ashes in it.

"You think I'm up to something," the FBI agent says, leaning back in his chair, smoke swirling around him. "You don't trust me. You are not a trusting person."

"I would not say I am a trusting person overall, no," says Viola, ashing.

"Furthermore, you believe in the importance of the confidentiality between a librarian and her patrons for the sake of a free society, whether said patrons have an interest in cookbooks or anarchism or porn or whatever else."

"Yes," says Viola.

"You're idealistic," the FBI agent says. "I love that. God, you're beautiful."

"I don't know what you're up to, but flattery's not going to work," Viola says, taking a long drag on her cigarette. "Anyhow I'm married."

"Well sure you're married. I noticed the ring," the FBI agent says, taking her by the wrist to examine it. "It's a really lovely ring. Men too often think that women want something ostentatious, something with a lot of diamonds."

"I'm against the diamond trade."

"Well sure you are. Injustice anywhere sickens you. A person can tell that just by looking at your face. Is it okay, me holding your wrist like this?"

"It's actually, um, it's actually a little uncomfortable. It's really, it kind of hurts, actually."

The FBI agent presses her wrist tighter.

"Let me tell you a story," he says. "It's a sort of parable, about the importance of stability and the secret law. When I was a kid I lived for a while on a military base in Germany. These three blond Germans nihilists would always hang around one of the cafés not far from the base. They were in their late teens or early twenties, all students, you know, avoiding real life as long as possible. One of them had a mohawk and wore an extra-large safety pin in his cheek. My father, the Chief Master Sergeant Michael H. Augusto, didn't like the looks of these guys, and he would tell them that whenever he passed them. In return for which they'd ask him all sorts of searching questions about life, which really got to him because, you know, he was a military man, he didn't have time to be thinking about all that. They were all like, 'Hey, how do you deal with the uncertainty of man's position in the *Welt*, in which he is simultaneously master *und* worm?' And he'd get so frustrated with them that he'd come home and push my mother into mirrors. We kept having to buy new mirrors, because he kept pushing my mother into them. There were mornings where there wasn't a single mirror in the house when you needed to brush your teeth or comb your hair. It was frustrating, never knowing if you were going to have a mirror to look into when you needed to comb your hair. And I was fourteen, just getting into girls, so that was a big deal, you know, at the time.

"And so one Saturday I sat at the café several seats down from them, and waited for them to walk back to the shabby little German apartment that they shared, and I kicked in their door and beat the three of them with a sock full of pennies. One of the nihilists, I broke his jaw and his nose, and the other two I put into the hospital with concussions."

"Jesus," Viola says.

"Do you understand what I am trying to tell you, here?"

"This is actually getting really painful," Viola says, blinking away tears. "This is actually, I'm worried that you might break my wrist."

"I'm not going to break your wrist," the FBI agent says, quiet and very close to her face. "Do you believe me? Do you believe that I'm not going to break your wrist?"

A long still moment. Viola nods.

"Good," the FBI agent says.

VIOLA COMES HOME to find Robert in his office, watching the instructional DVD on rough sex. "If I'm being one hundred percent honest, I don't understand why you would want this," Robert says to Viola.

"You mean, what's wrong with me?" Viola asks.

"I didn't say that." Robert follows Viola out of the office and into the kitchen, where Viola starts putting away dishes a little too quietly. "Could you try to understand why this is difficult for me? People don't naturally wish themselves harm."

Viola keeps putting away the dishes. Robert sits at the kitchen table. He is suddenly very tired.

"There's a difference between hurt and harm," Viola says.

"Okay," Robert says. "Which do you want?"

ROBERT GOES to a Mexican restaurant with his friend Trey, who works as a drug representative for Obadiah Birch, the pharmaceutical company Robert's firm represents. A large mariachi band is playing in one corner of the restaurant. The restaurant's hostess, a tiny blond with noticeable acne scars, winces every time the trumpets hit a high note. "Welcome to Fiesta Friday," she says, wincing. "Ándale to this table over here, compays." Their table's next to the band. The guitarist, a skinny, dark man with small, straight teeth, leers at the hostess.

"Amy, my love!"

"Antonio, shove it." She tosses their menus on the table. "Hope you don't mind the band. We can't sit parties with female members anywhere near them, not since Antonio's started his treatment for ADHD. Better than it used to be, though. At least he doesn't change keys fifteen times a song anymore."

The guitarist approaches Robert and Trey's table, still strumming. "That is totally unfair. Like, sirs, I may be the slightest bit passionate, which is one-hundred percent acceptable and even encouraged in the music biz, but I have never let that interfere with my art. Oh, let me introduce myself. Yo me llamo Antonio and this is the Tijuana Six. We are here most Fridays, and we sing about love, which all of us have some experience with, however painful or ill-fated."

"You don't really sound Mexican, you know," Trey observes.

"Oh we're from Northern Cali, mostly. Except for Hugo over there. He's Hungarian. But he *is* an illegal immigrant, if that makes you feel any more confidence in our authenticity as a mariachi band."

Hugo takes the trumpet from his lips and shrugs. "I am running from the military service."

"Do they have democracy over there yet?" asks Trey.

"Yes, as of March 1990."

"Well good to hear it."

They order bistec and enchiladas and Mexican beer which comes with a little sombrero-shaped bowls of limes. Robert messes with one of the extra limes, while the band plays softly nearby. "This one was the furthest along. I think that's part of it."

“I’m amazed by how well you’re taking all this.”

“Honestly, me too,” Robert says.

They order another round of beer.

“It’s just that it feels selfish sometimes, you know?” Robert says. “Like she wants to keep all the sadness to herself. I get that this is difficult on her, God knows. But it was my kid too. Sometimes I feel like she doesn’t even understand that. I am trying to be supportive.”

“It’s not unusual, in these sorts of traumatic situations, for conditions to manifest,” Trey says.

“I don’t think it’s a condition,” Robert says, louder than intended. “I think she’s being fucking selfish.” Robert looks down at his beer. “Sorry,” he says.

“Hey, buddy, it’s okay. I’m on your side here,” gripping one of Robert’s shoulders and giving it a squeeze. Robert exhales.

Robert has known Trey since high school, where they played football together, Robert as a center and Trey as a running back. They once pulled a counter-run in which Robert, along with the right guard and right tackle, blocked left, while Trey feinted to the left then cut to the right, grabbed the handoff, and shot through the hole created by the offensive line’s misdirection. It was a very good play.

"Love is a complex process," Trey explains. "A chemical process. A series of chemical processes, in the brain. Basically, a Rube-Goldberg machine of chemical interactions. Ridiculously complex. In purely physical terms, it is very easy for it to go wrong. There's a long list of ways it can go wrong, in fact, many of which we're currently researching: Obsessive Love Disorder, Hypersexuality, Hypoactive Desire Disorder. ED, of course. Erotic paranoia. Erotomania, also known as de Clérambault's syndrome. Sex and Love Addiction, Codependency. Erotophobia, genophobia, phallophobia. Female Sexual Arousal Disorder. Anorgasmia or Coughlan's syndrome. Vaginismus. Sexual Aversion Disorder. Love-shyness." Trey cocks his head to the side, clearly thinking. "I'm missing something, I'm sure. Anyhow, there are a lot. The problem is that love is so romanticized in Western culture that people don't even realize they can get help."

"Huh," says Robert.

The lights lower for the band's grand finale. Antonio, the mariachi guitarist, sings a song about his melancholy *amor*, whose melancholy forced her, quite against her will, to be *infiel*. His *amor*, he sings, was so melancholy and so *infiel* that in the end she died of her infinite sadness, which until that moment he had not known could be fatal. Hugo plays a funeral dirge on his trumpet. Trey motions for the check.

OUTSIDE THE WIND IS SO STRONG that bits of parking lot gravel and small stones fly through the air like hail, and Robert and Trey have to shield their faces and stumble half-blind to their cars. Trey calls out what Robert assumes must be a goodbye from across the parking lot, his words twisted by the wind into a series of sounds only just recognizable as human speech. Robert yells back and doesn't recognize his own voice in his ears.

BEYOND THE WINDOWS of Robert's car, the wind seems to assume shapes, even bodies with distinct personalities, that for a moment brush past, then dissipate, and are gone. Partway home Robert realizes that he doesn't have his wallet on him. By the time he makes it back to the restaurant the band has changed out of their mariachi outfits and is packing up for the night.

"Your wallet?" says the hostess. "Antonio found it," pointing. "Must've slipped out of your pocket." Robert checks: everything's still there.

"Hey, what are you drinking?" Robert asks Antonio, joining him and a couple of his bandmates at the bar. He buys the guitarist a whiskey neat and asks for a water for himself. "I'm driving," he explains.

"Here's to driving!" Antonio says, and he and his bandmates turn their glasses up.

"You have a real depth of sorrow to your voice when you sing, by the way," Robert says. "I meant to say that when I was here earlier. I think it's really admirable, how you can convey that."

"Well we're pretty broke all the time, and it's sad, not having money. I mean, have you tried being a professional musician? We play in these shit little restaurants—no offense, Amy," he says to the hostess, who ignores him, "—and just scrape by. Not a lot of money to be made, playing music. Hugo here guinea-pigs on the side."

Hugo shrugs. "I take some pills, they give me money. There are worse things."

"He only does it occasionally, mind you."

"One time I vomited every fifteen minutes for the duration of the study. That was a dark time. But I'm young, still."

"So you ran away from the military?" Robert says.

"It was a stupid thing to do. I'd heard that we were to be engaged in Afghanistan. But in the end, very few soldiers went. It seems I was too hasty."

"Do you like America?"

"Sure, there's a lot of freedom."

"How does it compare to Hungary?"

"About equal, in terms of freedom. Still, I have at times an overwhelming longing for the beauty of the northern Hungarian landscape."

“Oh boy, I know all about longing,” Antonio says, giving Hugo’s shoulder a friendly punch. “Amy, over there? Jesus, the longing that I have for her. Her hair is like flax. Isn’t her hair like flax? And her eyes are like little chips of something, like something that’s been chipped off . . . ”

“I used to be in a band,” says Robert. “I played drums. We played the Vogue, here in Indianapolis.”

“There’s not much use for a drummer in a mariachi band,” says Hugo, frowning. “It is not the tradition.”

"I STILL CARE about you very much," Viola says, in bed with him that night. "I think it's important for you to know that."

Robert continues facing the wall on his side of the bed. "I know."

THE FBI AGENT emails Viola. “What were you thinking about the first time you masturbated?” he writes. Viola stares at the screen of her laptop, then closes it.

ROBERT'S FATHER CALLS to tell him about the hallucinations that his grandmother has started having. "She's at the hospital now. But they can't find anything wrong with her. She's in perfect health, except for the hallucinations. They said maybe it has to do with her salt, that she wasn't getting enough of it."

"Salt?" says Robert.

"Apparently that can cause that. Not enough salt."

Robert goes to visit his grandmother, in the suburbs. She lives in a lovely house in a development that began during the boom and was never completed, because the housing market tanked. Empty lots are scattered throughout the neighborhood. Still, the houses that were finished have all been sold, and her neighbors, from what Robert knows of them, are reasonably friendly.

"I heard things were a bit rough earlier this week," Robert says.

Robert's grandmother leads him into the living room by the arm. "They made such a fuss out of everything. I don't think it was at all *necessary*."

Robert's grandmother sits in one of the two beautifully upholstered, uncomfortable chairs underneath a watercolor painting of trees. She seems to be confused about the salt thing. "They told me there I needed to watch my salt," she says. "But I don't eat hardly any salt. I'm very careful about that."

"They said you needed more salt, Grandmother," Robert says.

"Is that what they said?"

Robert changes into his shorts and running shoes and goes for a run. He traces the entirety of the housing development, running down each of its branches, circling around the cul-de-sac that tips each, running back. Uncompleted houses sit, half-built, an air of expectancy gathering around them, as though construction halted just an hour before and will resume at any moment. Cars slow down as they pass. The drivers, most of them elderly, wave.

Later that evening, Robert's grandmother asks him how many people are in the house. Robert is sitting on the couch in the living room, reading the thin local paper. He tells her, carefully, that it's just the two of them. He feels suddenly disoriented. Without quite thinking it, he gets the feeling that he might somehow be wrong, that she might have access to some knowledge he doesn't. The skin at the back of his neck crawls.

"Where's your father?"

"He's at his house, in Geist," Robert says. Robert's grandmother peers around the room, then her focus comes to rest on a spot on the couch somewhere to Robert's left.

"Who's that?" she says. "I don't like him."

Robert stares at the empty spot.

"Him," his grandmother says, waving her hand at it violently.

Robert's parents arrive. "I don't know what to do with her," Robert says.

"Let's get her into bed," Robert's father says. Robert and his father attempt to lead her from the couch into her bedroom. It goes fine for the first several steps, and then Robert's grandmother refuses to go any further. She insists that there's a hole in the carpet, right in front of her.

"A pit," she moans. "A pit."

"There's no pit there, Grandmother," Robert says. "It's just your carpet."

“What are you trying to do to me?” she asks. So Robert and his father lead her around the pit and into her bedroom.

“Should we call the paramedics?” Robert asks.

His grandmother insists that she is staying right where she is. “I don’t know what you are trying to do to me, but I am staying here.” The paramedics, when they arrive, come storming into the house, confident broad-shouldered men bearing medical equipment. One shines a light into her eye.

“This happened once before,” Robert’s father says. “Earlier this week. They said it was salt.”

“Salt?” asks a paramedic, his blunt healthy fingers tenderly feeling Robert’s grandmother’s wrist for the pulse.

“At the hospital. They couldn’t find anything wrong with her. But they said that not enough salt—”

“I’m not leaving,” Robert’s grandmother says, to the paramedics. “I do *not* want you in my house.”

“We’re just making sure you’re okay, ma’am,” the paramedic says. “Your son and your grandson here were concerned about you, is all. They say you’ve been having some hallucinations.”

“I have been doing no such thing.”

The paramedic asks her name, the year, who the

current president is. She hesitates a little on the last question, but eventually gets it right.

"You can't do anything for her?" Robert's father says.

"She's conscious, and coherent," the paramedic says. "If she says she doesn't want to go, we can't make her go."

Robert sits with his mother and father in the living room, around the glass-topped coffee table. His grandmother has finally gone to sleep. "Your mother thinks she's making it up," Robert's father says.

"I don't think she's making it up," Robert's mother says. "I just—Did you see how fast she came out of it, as soon as the paramedics got here? Just like that, and she was totally coherent."

"Probably it was adrenaline," Robert says. "Probably it was a shock to her system, all those strangers in her house, all at once."

"I just think," Robert's mother says. "Well, all of her friends are getting sick now, and she sees how much attention they're getting . . . "

"I think it's all the pills she's on," Robert's father says. "She keeps getting them confused, recently."

"If it was that, don't you think they'd have found out about it at the hospital?" Robert's mother says, in a sharp whisper.

"She's asleep," Robert's father says. "You don't have to whisper."

"Oh, I don't know what she is," Robert's mother says.

ROBERT VOLUNTEERS to stay the night, to make sure that his grandmother is okay. He makes himself a bed on the couch in the living room, his head a few feet from the door to her room. He thinks about pits that suddenly open up in the floor. He thinks about the possibility that there could be other people, other voices, swirling in the room around him, invisible.

"Robert," calls his grandmother softly, during the night. "Robert." Robert walks into her room and stands beside her bed. Her small fragile hand grips his. "Robert, I was just playing," she says. "You believe me, don't you. Robert I don't want you letting those men in my house anymore."

ROBERT AND VIOLA meet with Robert's parents to discuss the question of Robert's grandmother. Robert's father, who is retiring as a partner from his firm this year, tells Viola that she looks lovely and asks if she's heard the one about the talking Mexican cigar. Viola, who has always had a soft spot for Robert's distant and surprisingly awkward father, smiles and says that she has not.

Robert, Viola, and Robert's parents sit around Robert's parents' kitchen table in Geist, in the suburbs. Robert's younger brother, who does IT for a company in Houston, is on speakerphone. "Hello?" Robert's brother says.

"Coming in loud and clear," Robert's father says.

"Hello?" says Robert's brother.

Robert's mother says she thinks that it's time to seriously consider the possibility of an elderly care facility. "I know we've been putting this off as long as we can," she says. "And ultimately of course it isn't up to me."

Robert's grandmother has come to believe that there is a tremendous emptiness underneath her house that might swallow her at any moment. "Do they still think it's the salt?" Robert asks.

"They don't know what it is. She's old," Robert's mother says.

"She's in perfect health," says Robert's father.

"Except for the hallucinations," Robert's mother says. "Honestly, you would think she would *want* to move."

A staticky crashing sound comes through over the speakerphone. "I'm okay," says Robert's brother. "I was trying to replace a light bulb, but I'm okay."

"Did you fall? Are you hurt?" Robert's mother wants to know.

"You okay, champ?"

"Hello?" says Robert's brother.

"I feel like if she doesn't want to go she shouldn't go," Viola says.

"How do you clean up these compact fluorescents?" Robert's brother asks. "You just like sweep it up? Is that safe?"

"I'm looking it up on my phone right now baby," Robert's mother says.

"Hello?"

Robert's parents wave to Robert and Viola as they pull out of the driveway, the cellphone containing Robert's brother's voice held aloft in the air to indicate that he, too, is saying goodbye. "Are they happy?" Viola asks. "Your parents."

Robert gives this some thought. "I think maybe you put too much emphasis on being happy," he says. "People don't always have to be happy."

"I don't see why it's such a big thing to ask."

They stop at a drug store on the way home to pick up headache medicine for the headaches Robert has been getting recently. "There are things more important in life than happiness sometimes," Robert says, scanning the aisle.

"Like what?"

"Like family. Or ethical convictions. Or helping others."

"Don't those things make you happy? Isn't that the point?"

At home that night, Viola looks through old photo albums of Robert in college, his almost uniformly blond friends, well-tanned, girls bikini'd and with lovely teeth, some of them of course Robert's exes, not all of them, some percentage that Viola has not taken the time to calculate. What beach is this, Viola thinks, that they seem always to be on, somehow, in Indiana? Who wouldn't be happy with this life, Viola thinks, this blond, well-formed husband?

VIOLA WRITES BACK to the FBI agent: "The first time I masturbated I was eleven. I don't think I understood what I was doing, then. As far as I can remember I wasn't thinking about anything in particular, but I remember feeling slightly ashamed because I was touching myself."

The FBI agent writes to Viola: "Please answer the questions exactly as they are asked. If I require additional information I will tell you."

Viola writes to the FBI agent: "When I fantasize, I fantasize about faceless men, or men I don't recognize. Like, I specifically don't recognize them in the fantasies. Sometimes their faces are covered in shadows, or are grotesque in such a way that I am unsure, in the fantasy, whether or not they are wearing a mask. These fantasies often involve some degree of violence or coercion, though of course I find violence in real life repugnant."

VIOLA GOES OUT with her friend Bethany to a bar with a small dance floor near the back. Viola is acting as "wingman" for her friend Bethany. Whenever any men come up to her to ask if she'd like a drink, Viola says, "I am the wingman. This is my friend Bethany."

"You're a mighty pretty little wingman."

"Thank you."

"Would you like a cigarette?"

"Okay."

"How about a dance?"

"You don't want to dance with me," Viola says, accepting a light for her cigarette. "I'm terrible. Legs and arms all over the place. Dance partners seriously injured, on more than one occasion. I've put men in casts. Now my friend Bethany, on the other hand..."

Viola and Bethany sit at the bar looking out at the dance floor. A tiny disco ball spins near the ceiling, scattering light across the dancers. One short and hirsute man in particular buzzes from partner to partner, as if gathering pollen from each. "I think one of the problems with growing up as a kid who spent basically all of her time reading is that it's hard to accept the idea that this single life is all you get," Viola says. "You get so used to the idea of a narrative arc to things, of life as a sort of meaningful unit, of being able to switch from one life to another and from one head to another. And on some level you begin to think that that's how things actually are, that you can try something out, and if you don't like it, you can just switch. That at some point you get to be everything. Then suddenly you're twenty five years old, thirty, and you realize that you only actually get one life and one head to be inside of."

Bethany gives her a look.

"Well, okay, I *realized* it before. Like, logically speaking, yes. I'm talking about, just . . . just this *sense*, not really at the level of thought, but the sense that the world works more like books than like, you know, the world."

Viola and Bethany talk to a pair of men who claim to be airline pilots. Viola introduces herself with a fake name. "Have you ever almost crashed?" she asks.

"Flying is actually a very safe means of travel," the handsomer of the two says. He is wearing a black tie with a tight blue shirt with a little bit of stretch to it, which shows off his physique nicely.

"What's the closest you've ever come to crashing? Did you announce it? Did the little things pop out from overhead? The masks."

The handsome pilot looks at her, concerned, then turns to give Bethany a smile.

Robert is already in bed by the time Viola gets home that night. He tells her she smells like smoke. "Of course I smell like smoke," she says. "It was a bar. People were smoking. Jesus, Robert."

"Are you drunk?"

Viola struggles to get off one of her shoes, nearly falling backwards in the process. "I'm tipsy."

Viola gets off the other shoe, then awkwardly pulls off her tights. She clambers into bed beside him and starts pawing at Robert's chest. "I don't want to do this right now," Robert says.

"You are my husband," Viola says. "My well-formed husband and I would like you to fuck me."

Robert goes to get Viola a glass of water.

"Jesus, Robert," Viola says when he returns. "I don't want to break up. I don't want us to just be *done*, Jesus. Is that what you think I want?"

“Here, drink,” Robert says.

“What time is it,” Viola says, taking the glass. “Jesus.”

ROBERT LOOKS UP IMAGES of bathroom sinks on his computer at work. He's thinking about getting rid of the countertops in the bathroom entirely and replacing them with a pedestal sink. He looks through several blocky modernist pedestal sink designs. Maybe something more classical, he thinks.

Interns mill about the offices, becoming more sure of their future success with every passing day.

At home Robert shuts off the water supply to the bathroom sink and uses a crescent wrench to disconnect the water lines. He then disconnects the drain pipe and removes the sink from the countertop. He looks for the screws that should connect the countertop to the cabinet. Try as he might, he can't find how it is connected. He re-reads the instructions that he printed off the internet. The instructions do not offer any insight as to where the screws that attach the countertop to the cabinet should be located. One would assume somewhere around the edges. Finally Robert just tugs at it in frustration. The whole cabinet comes away from the wall.

"There seems to be quite a bit of water damage behind the cabinet," Robert calls out. "Viola?" But she is not home.

Robert looks up "what to do about water damage" on the internet. The results are not encouraging. "I'm going to have to replace this bit of drywall," Robert calls out. He drives to the hardware store and buys a strip of drywall and a roll of fiberglass mesh and premixed joint compound and a drywall saw.

Using the drywall saw Robert cuts out an approximately three-foot by three-foot square around the damaged section of drywall. "That's strange," Robert says. He goes to get a flashlight. "I can't see the opposite wall," Robert calls out, even though he's pretty sure that Viola still isn't home. He crawls through the hole, holding the flashlight beam steady in front of him, and finds that, once inside the wall, he can stand up. It's an old house, Robert thinks, there are bound to be some surprises. Still, after living here with Viola for four years, you would think that we knew the place pretty well. Robert walks through the darkness, flashlight beam shining off into the distance, trying to figure out exactly where, in the home's layout, he is. The air feels deathly still. There are not, as far as he can tell, any spiderwebs, there don't seem to be any insects or animals at all. The ground is flat, featureless, and is the only thing he can see other than the hole in the drywall, receding farther and farther into the distance. Robert feels empty. The emptiness feels like a secret.

"If I keep walking, will I find anything?" he says.

"No," says the emptiness. "This is the space reserved in every house for emptiness. It is a space that cannot be filled."

"Once I patch up the wall, this space will continue to exist," Robert says.

"Correct," says the emptiness.

"And this is the space that consumes all of our efforts to fix things, to make them right."

"Also correct."

Robert sits down on the featureless ground and turns off the flashlight. "And if I decide to stay here?"

"You will be consumed in the emptiness. You will become part of it. This is already beginning to happen, as you have noticed. There is a yawning emptiness inside you at this very moment."

Robert closes his eyes, opens them, closes them again. There is no difference, of course.

WHEN ROBERT CLOSES his eyes to sleep that night, the darkness that he sees is no longer darkness, it is an expanding emptiness. He tries to find the end of it, with no success. The further you go, he thinks, the more emptiness there is. It can just keep going, he thinks. There's no reason to think it stops.

"PRAIRIE VOLES," Robert's friend Trey says. "Let's talk about prairie voles."

"Okay," Robert says.

Robert is sitting on Trey's slick black leather couch and Trey is sitting in the matching armchair. Between them there is a stylish black table and on top of the table is a little baggie of pills. The furniture and walls throughout Trey's house are dark and give one the impression they were ordered, as a set, from a men's magazine.

"Prairie voles mate for life," Trey says. "They do all kinds of really sweet and disgusting things for each other once they've mated for life, like for example grooming each other and making soft comforting prairie-vole noises to each other in their nest. This is because they have an unusual number of receptors in their brain for the chemicals oxytocin and vasopressin. Other species of voles do not have these receptors, and they have no problem leaving their mates at the first convenient opportunity. They don't have even the slightest interest in grooming or making soft comforting noises to voles they've mated with. Now, if you were a biologist working with voles, and you turned down the amount of oxytocin and vasopressin inside a prairie vole brain, do you know what? Suddenly they have no interest in grooming or making soft comforting noises to each other either, and they just go wandering off to find the next available vole."

"I'm not even sure what a vole is," Robert says.

"Like a small rat," says Trey. "They're not especially charming."

On one wall there are pictures of Trey in high school in his football uniform and there is a picture of Robert and Trey's entire high-school football team and there is a small photograph of Trey's ex-wife and daughter. The daughter is four or five in the photograph, and has messy blond hair. The ex-wife and daughter live somewhere in California.

Trey shows Robert the bottle of fortified pinotage that he brought back with him from his recent physicians' conference in South Africa. He pours out two glasses. The pinotage tastes like fruit juice concentrate with undertones of paint. "A lot of people say that," Trey says. "It can take a little while to develop an appreciation for its subtleties."

Trey talks to Robert about the potential adverse effects of the pills, which are currently in Phase II clinical trials. The potential adverse effects are point-one percent seizure, point oh-two percent neuroleptic malignant syndrome, three percent confusion, eleven percent dry mouth, fourteen to seventeen percent decreased appetite, four percent headache, five percent akathisia, seven percent other symptoms. "Those are all very low percents," Robert says.

"It's a very safe drug." Trey refills their glasses. He notes that the pills dissolve pretty much instantly in liquid.

"I try to write my daughter letters sometimes," Trey says. "Mostly this is at night when I've had too much to drink, but not always. I have, at last estimate, tried to write her dozens and dozens of letters, with no success. When I read what I've written, even the salutations seem wrong. 'Dear Kimberly,' 'Dearest Kimberly,' 'Dear Kim,' 'Baby'—you can see how difficult it is. She's just turned twelve, three weeks ago. She calls me every year on my birthday and we talk, sometimes for as long as an hour. Other than that I see her at Christmas."

Trey takes Robert into his office to show him his new humidor. "That looks quite elegant."

"Solid Spanish Cedar. A little computerized system keeps the humidity inside at precisely seventy percent. Manufactured by the German company Gerl Manufactur."

"I didn't know you smoked cigars."

"I don't, I just keep them because I like the smell. This is a Cohiba and this is a hand-made Ramon Allones Gigante and this is a Davidoff 'Zino.' "

"That's quite a collection."

"Thank you."

ROBERT SPENDS a long time staring at the plastic baggie of pills that his friend Trey gave him.

I PRIDE MYSELF on being a good person, Robert thinks. Perhaps to my detriment. What good is my goodness doing? What good is it doing either of us?

Robert gathers together a cutting board and a knife and some cilantro and an onion and places them all on the island in the middle of the kitchen. Viola is at work. Robert cooks some small strips of beef in a skillet. He places one of the pills on the cutting board and crushes it to a powder with the side of the knife. He wets the tip of his finger and touches it to the powder and tastes it. It doesn't taste like anything.

Robert gets down a wine glass from the rack that hangs above the kitchen counter and pours himself a glass of wine. He sips the wine and dices the cilantro and the onion. He checks the small strips of beef in the skillet, then gets some tortillas from the refrigerator and heats them in a pan on the stove. He sips the wine and waits for the tortillas and the beef.

He thinks about the night in law school when he and several members of his cohort, all slightly drunk, drove to Kokomo, Indiana, where, they had been assured, there was a whorehouse right by the cemetery. None of them actually wanted or intended to sleep with a whore. It was like a big joke between them all, he's pretty sure, though none of them would admit they weren't serious. When they got to Kokomo they parked near the graveyard and got out cans of beer from the case in the trunk and wandered around, laughing and shushing each other. It's a wonder they weren't arrested. If they had ever found the place, if such a place existed, what would they have done? He supposes they would have gone inside, and felt uncomfortable, and each found some excuse to leave.

The kitchen fills with the smell of beef and warm tortillas. Robert wipes the crushed-up pill from the cutting board into his hand and sprinkles it into the wineglass. He tops off the wine. The powder has dissolved completely. Once again, there's no discernible taste.

He puts the tortillas on a plate and tops them with the beef, diced onions, and cilantro, and carries the plate and the wineglass into the next room. On the television is more news about the shootings that have been taking place in downtown Indianapolis. All of the victims so far have been researchers connected with Obadiah Birch. Shots of empty downtown lots crisscrossed with police tape while the reporters talk. Robert changes the channel to a sports program about March Madness. A man Robert doesn't recognize says, "Kansas doesn't have a prayer this year." Another man says, "Kansas does indeed have a prayer this year." Robert finishes his plate of tortillas and stares at the swallow of wine still in his glass. He puts down the plate and takes the wine to the kitchen and pours it down the sink. He takes the baggie of pills from his pocket and puts them in the trashcan under the sink. He feels better. He rinses out his glass and pours himself some more wine and goes back to the den to watch the rest of the sports program.

That night Robert watches his wife, asleep, and feels a great chasm opening between them. He thinks about unintended adverse effects, such-and-such percentage of decreased appetite, such-and-such percentage of dry mouth, such-and-such of confusion. He gets up from bed, quietly, so as not to disturb Viola, and goes downstairs and gets on his knees by the trashcan under the sink and fishes the baggie of pills back out. He looks at them for a long time.

Instead, he decides they should go to Italy.

"Italy!" he says the next evening, when Viola gets home.

"What?" Viola says.

"Italy! I just bought us tickets."

"When were you going to ask me about this?"

"We can rent a small European car and drive around the countryside, taking in the beauty of the Italian landscape. In such surroundings our love cannot help but grow and grow."

"I just got back from medical leave," Viola says.

"É bella e piacente, l'Italia," Robert says. "They will be understanding. They will, they will."

Viola thinks: Is there a fresh start for us, in Italy?

Robert flies to Italy, alone.

ROBERT WRITES to Viola from Italy:

Today in a café on the river I saw a young woman of extraordinary beauty. She appeared to be studying mathematics—she had what looked like a textbook with her, and was shaking her head while writing out long strings of numbers on a pad of paper. The standard sheet of paper here is longer than ours, almost what we call "legal size." It occurred to me that that extra amount of paper might make her computations that much more overwhelming, a page filled with even more numbers. Would she, mostly likely unfamiliar with our smaller American-sized paper, still somehow feel that difference? That tiny additional bit of overwhelmingness? But perhaps she enjoys mathematics, many people do—I myself feel generally comfortable with numbers, though

I never liked those higher math classes where I couldn't see any possible application for the concepts we learned.

I have kept up my running here. Each day I manage greater and greater distances, and feel swelling within me a sense of accomplishment. Once while running in a piazza filled with birds I nearly crashed into a man selling dried corn to tourists. He ran after me for several blocks, attempting to convince me that he should be recompensed for the corn that spilled when I nearly ran into him. I argued back, as best as I could while continuing to run, and made signs of my innocence. I do not believe, to be honest, that he had spilled much corn; it was merely that he had taken me for a tourist . . .

The Italian people in general, as portrayed in films and television, are of a warm and open disposition. Many of them want to discuss American politics with me, a subject about which I am I think reasonably hesitant. I have ventured far out into the Tuscan countryside. My high-school Italian, though rusty, has served me well. My rather more proficient Latin less so, ha ha.

The world is so big. Even the tiny part of it that we see in a single lifetime is so big.

Your Robert.

PS. I love you and I believe you when you tell me that you care about me. What other choice do I have?

DOES
NOT
LOVE

"I DON'T WANT YOU to kiss me," Viola says to the FBI agent. "That is a hard boundary for me, I think."

"No kissing," the FBI agent says. "Anything else?"

"Could you turn that light down a little bit? Just for right now, anyway."

"The light has only two settings," the FBI agent explains. "On or off."

"Well could you turn it away, at least? It's making my head hurt."

Viola is sitting in a straightbacked chair in a motel room in Danville, a town maybe twenty minutes outside of Indianapolis. The FBI agent has moved the motel-room desk so that it faces Viola's chair, and he sits on the other side of it. He adjusts the light.

Viola crosses her legs and tugs down at her skirt.

"Do you like being humiliated?" the FBI agent asks. Viola gives it some thought.

"In certain controlled situations."

"What was the time that you were most sexually aroused, that you can remember?"

Viola tells him.

"So not with your husband."

"I don't want to talk about my husband with you."

"You don't feel comfortable talking about your husband with me."

"I just don't see why he has to be a subject of conversation is all."

The FBI agent handcuffs Viola's hands behind the back of the chair. "Do you remember your safeword?" the FBI agent asks. Viola nods. The FBI agent slaps her. She cannot tell if he has an erection. She can barely see him, in fact, except as a shadowy figure just beyond the light.

"Do you love your husband?" the FBI agent asks.

Viola's safeword is the word "safeword," which she chose because it seemed kind of funny, or noncommittal, maybe. She works the edges of the handcuffs with her fingers.

"I care for him very deeply," Viola says.

The FBI agent slaps her. "Please answer the question as it is asked. Do you love your husband?"

"I think sometimes that I love him very much. At other times I am sure that I do not. The sureness of my not-loving him, at those times, seems to retroactively negate whatever love I once believed myself to hold, and I think to myself: I have never loved him, that was a mistake, I was only wanting to love him."

"Have you loved other men?"

"I had a series of relationships before Robert, some of which felt at the time as though they constituted love. Looking back, I find it hard to believe that love was involved. Many of them, retrospectively, feel like they consisted of a certain mutual neediness."

The FBI agent holds Viola down on the mattress by the throat. There is some fumbling with his fly. Viola thinks: I am not supposed to help him with his fly, I am being held down, I am "at his mercy." The FBI agent spits on Viola and Viola closes her eyes in anticipation of being spat on again.

THE FBI AGENT is living out of a suitcase in the motel room in Danville. The motel room has a bed with pale green sheets and a cheap-looking desk and chair. It's all clean and a little sad. Viola tries to imagine what his actual home is like, but she can't. Maybe he just moves from motel room to motel room, forever.

THERE IS AN AIR of menace to the FBI agent. It is not exactly in the things that he does—or rather, if it is, it is hard to pin down exactly what those things are. Menace seems to adhere to him, as a quality.

It is cultivated, he tells Viola. The air of menace is a part of the job.

"That doesn't make it any less menacing," Viola says.

"Is it a problem?"

"No, I think I like it," Viola says. "In a lover. I don't think that I would want to live with it."

"I see," the FBI agent says, then begins to sulk. He sulks greatly, while for example tying Viola to the motel room bed. He even sulks while having sex with her. At first it is funny, but then after a while it's too much. He is temperamental, Viola thinks, not for the first time. He has a sensitive soul. The soul, perhaps, of an artist.

"How do you cultivate it? The air of menace," Viola asks, intending this as a sort of peace offering.

There are ten basic methods, the FBI agent tells her, though of course individual agents are free to come up with their own variations. "Method number one: The scowl. It should not be a simple, straightforward, or otherwise thuggish scowl. It should contain elements of both disappointment and resolution. One should look as though one is scowling in spite of one's own inclinations, that one would rather not be scowling but that one recognizes the necessity of the scowl. It should be clear, in other words, that the necessity of the scowl arises from circumstances outside of oneself.

"Method number two: The question of what to do with one's arms. This is a difficult one; fidgeting of any sort betrays weakness. Many people, in attempting to portray an air of menace, will cross the arms in front of the torso. That is incorrect. It telegraphs to the target one's own insecurity, that one must so forcefully project confidence. Much better to keep one's arms at one's sides, loose and ready. Rather than mask fidgeting, one demonstrates thereby that one simply isn't going to fidget.

"Method number three: Cleanliness. Method

number three-b: Clean-shavenness. Methods number four through eight, classified. Method number nine: Righteousness. One should never give the appearance of so much as a moment of self-doubt. It should be clear that any violence that one is to visit upon the other, no matter how distasteful personally (see method one), is absolutely necessary from a grander perspective. Method number ten: Dark, freshly-pressed suits."

THE FBI AGENT likes to videotape her when they have sex, holding the camcorder in one hand and pinning down her wrists with the other. At times the lens is just inches from her face. She should not be enjoying this as much as she does, she thinks. But she does. She finds herself noticing security cameras in public places, like grocery stores and home furnishing stores, and thinking of his body pressed down on hers. There are moments while they're fucking when it seems totally reasonable to mistake the camcorder for his face, to think that the acts of fucking and recording are one and the same.

VIOLA, BORED, begins looking through the contents of the FBI agent's suitcase. "Don't do that."

Underneath a layer of shirts identical to the one he's currently wearing, Viola finds stacks of VHS tapes, each labeled with the date, time, and a set of coordinates. She smirks. "So these are all other girls?"

"No, they're not."

"Look, you don't need to worry about me getting jealous. I am totally not interested in being jealous."

"They're not."

"What are they then?"

The FBI agent tells her that it would be better for her sake if she didn't know.

"What, this is like a national security thing?"

"No, I just think you'd be happier not knowing."

Viola pouts. "You don't have to worry about hiding other women from me. I like the idea that you've fucked other women. I like thinking that you're fucking them all the time. Like, if I turn my back, suddenly there'll be another woman in the room, and you'll be fucking her. Like this." Viola does an impression of the FBI agent fucking another woman, his mouth curled up in a snarl, his eyes slit comically.

"Don't mock me," he says.

"I wasn't mocking you."

"What you were doing with your face. It was mocking me."

"What, this?" Viola starts, but then sees his expression and thinks better of it. "Why don't you show me how you'd really do it, then?" she says, pulling him towards her.

"WHY ARE YOU really here?" Viola asks the FBI agent. They are lying under the pale green sheets.

"I'm really here to spy on you, personally. We have determined that you represent one of the primary threats to our national security."

"Knew it," Viola says.

"The present administration recognizes that sadness runs counter to our way of life," the FBI agent says. "And yet you keep insisting on being sad."

Viola turns away from him to face the wall. "I already said I'm over it. How many times do I have to tell you? Besides, that doesn't make any sense, insisting on being sad. I don't insist on anything."

ROBERT RETURNS FROM his vacation in Italy with a small image of Catherine of Alexandria, patron saint of archivists, librarians, and apologists, which had been blessed by the new pope. "It's very pretty," Viola says, rubbing her finger over the image in its gold locket.

Viola looks up St. Catherine in a new edition of the *Lives of the Saints*, Dewey Decimal classification 120, Theology. Catherine's fame centers on her attempted conversion of the Emperor Maxentius, who, in response, first tortured and imprisoned her, then, when Catherine remained steadfast in her faith, attempted to marry her. The virgin Catherine of course replied that she was betrothed to Christ, an answer that so enraged Maxentius that he tortured her again, this time with a giant spiked wheel. The wheel miraculously flew apart in response to Catherine's prayers, at which point

Maxentius decided to behead her. Modern scholars note that the earliest accounts of Catherine's life date to five hundred years after her death, and that there is little to no evidence of her existence as a historic personage. In addition to librarians, archivists, and apologists, the *Lives* notes that she is patron to "millers, potters, spinners, knife-sharpeners, and other persons who work with a wheel." She is often represented in paintings as a scholar.

Viola looks at the ways her body has stretched from the last several pregnancies. There is a spiderweb of stretch marks across her hips and stomach. If this were for something, she thinks. If this were a sign of something tangible. I can imagine looking down at my body and being proud of what it has done. Holding my child and looking down at the signs of my strong body. But all it has done is spit out failure.

Other times she thinks: This is what I have survived. That itself is worth being proud of.

Does the FBI agent find this sexy, she thinks. Of course he's noticed. You can't not notice. How does he interpret these marks on her body? Is it a thing for him? A fetish? She doesn't like the idea of it being a fetish, though she's not entirely sure why. What ultimately is the difference between a fetish and simply being attracted to something that other people aren't?

Robert of course loves her too much for her to ever get the truth out of him.

VIOLA'S TALK THERAPIST has new plants. They look better than the old plants. Warmer, somehow. Viola tries to remember if the old plants were fake, and can't.

"I didn't think I was settling, with Robert," Viola says to the talk therapist. "I thought that there were certain things about the relationship that I was very excited about, and other things that I was less excited about but thought that I could live with. Isn't that true of every relationship?"

"Do you think it's significant that you keep avoiding discussing your miscarriage?"

"Miscarriages," Viola says. "Three. And how long could I possibly talk about them?"

Viola's talk therapist recommends that she start keeping lists of things that she's grateful for. Viola writes down: Apples. Newly-fallen leaves. The smell of crayons. Bright colors. Internet videos of kittens and other small animals. She looks at her list and thinks, Saccharine. She tears the list out of the spiral-bound notebook she had been writing in and throws it away. She writes, at the top of a fresh sheet of paper: Things That I Am Grateful For. She stares at the sheet for a long time. It occurs to her that the exercise is designed to be saccharine, that the whole idea is to make her a more saccharine and thus more socially-acceptable person.

Viola has bruises on her body but won't tell Robert where they are from. According to the internet it's possible that she's bruising because she's not getting enough iron.

Robert goes to the grocery store and looks at the iron supplements. In the grocery store he reads a story about how a certain fungus can get into an ant's brain and take control of its entire motor system, thus causing the ant to act in ways going against the ant's self-interest. He buys a small bottle of iron supplements and the magazine with the story about the ants.

Robert calls his grandmother from the grocery store parking lot and asks about her salt, whether she's getting enough of it.

"Robert, it is always so good to hear your voice. How long has it been since you called?"

On the radio during the drive home a reporter

talks about the most recent shooting downtown.

This is number four.

ROBERT AND VIOLA discuss the nature of love.

"There are stages," Robert says. "The first stage is infatuation. It is primarily chemical in nature. It is perfectly natural, after a time, for this stage to fade."

"I could fall back in love with you," Viola says. "That is an option."

"How would you do that?"

"I don't know," Viola says. "I suppose it would just have to happen." They are sitting at the kitchen table, eating breakfast. Robert is eating oatmeal with almonds and molasses, and Viola is eating two pieces of toast.

"Are your concerns primarily sexual in nature? Do you need new adventures? Do you feel as though you are stagnating?"

"Is anything primarily sexual in nature?"

"Though you wouldn't deny that there have been issues."

"The purpose of love," Viola says, "from an evolutionary standpoint, is to keep two people together long enough to raise a kid. Of course, there are some pretty compelling arguments for why one should take evolutionary psychology with a grain of salt."

"It's not my fault that we haven't been able to have a kid."

"Whose fault is it?"

"It's nobody's fault. Why does there need to be fault?"

"One of our bodies has had to put up with this," Viola says. "This constant failure."

"Is that what this is about?"

"I don't know what it's about."

Viola takes her plate to the sink to rinse it. She thinks: When we were first married, I thought that you were a well of stability, in which I could drown.

Viola places her plate in the dishwasher. She says, "There's no reason why two adults who get along reasonably well can't cohabitate, regardless of whether they are actively in love."

"Is that what you want?" Robert says. "Cohabitation?"

"The current scientific consensus is that love is not a single feeling, but a related cluster of feelings. Though we assume love to be unquestionably a good, studies have found that people in love spend more time sad, or angry, or in other forms of emotional distress than people not in love."

"I can't imagine a point in my life when I would not love you," Robert says, looking down at his bowl.

ROBERT AND VIOLA have dinner with Trey and his date at a new restaurant. All we ever do is go to new places, Viola thinks. The constant churn of the new. Once, newness was invigorating. Now, I am not sure if I could identify the difference between one new place and another.

"Nice to meet you," Viola says to Trey's date.

"Oh, we've met before," she says. "Viola, right?"

At the restaurant everyone around them seems to be talking about the secret law. "We are surrounded by enemies," says one older man sitting to Viola's right.

"The forces of disorder in all of its many forms," says his companion.

"Increasing disorder is the fundamental state of the universe," says a loud young man, several tables away. "Certain actions are necessary to prevent the encroaching of disorder—sometimes horrible actions—actions, that were they publically known, might themselves increase disorder. Actions which must therefore remain concealed. This is the particular insight of the secret law."

"Jesus," says Viola.

"Robert tells me that there's an FBI agent at your library these days," Trey says.

"I'm not allowed to talk about it," Viola says.

"NSL?" says Trey. Viola makes a zipping motion over her lips.

Appetizers arrive, in a series of small beautiful bowls.

"I am an optimist," Trey declares. "I believe in the basic goodness and order of the universe."

"So you are against the secret law?" Robert asks.

"I believe in the disease theory of crime," Trey says. "Containment, education. Ultimately, I think, we'll find biological bases for most forms of criminality."

"No free will?" Viola asks.

"Why would you want it?" Trey says, his chopsticks hovering above the bowls.

Somewhere around the main course Viola and Robert end up in a fight. No one is sure how it happens, not even Robert and Viola. They are fighting about the secret law, which Robert is in favor of and Viola opposes, except that really they are fighting about the fact that Robert suspects Viola is having an affair.

"Where do you think we'd end up, if anyone could do just anything and not have to worry about the consequences?" Robert says.

"I'm not saying there shouldn't be consequences," Viola says. "I'm saying that there shouldn't be terrible, unforeseeable consequences, carried out in secrecy by men who officially do not exist."

They are still fighting during the drive home.

"I'm not choosing to feel the way I feel in order to hurt you," Viola says.

"You know what I think?" Robert says. "I think you like the drama of it. I think instead of dealing with your actual feelings you've decided to make this into some big relationship drama."

"My 'actual feelings,'" Viola says, making it clear from her tone that she finds the phrase suspect. "I don't like seeing a therapist, Robert. But I am. Because I am an adult. And I am swallowing my pride and dealing with my 'actual feelings' and my mental fucking health like an adult."

"I'm fine," Robert says. "I'm not the one who's—I'm fine."

They pass adult stores, a mostly abandoned mall, kids too young to still be out walking along the soft shoulder of the road.

"Who are you fucking?" Robert says.

"Robert, Jesus."

"If you want to leave you should just leave."

So Viola leaves. She throws open the door at a stoplight and pushes herself out of the car just before the light turns green. Robert is so angry that he accelerates anyway, and drives two blocks with the passenger-side door open. He thinks, I could just drive off. He thinks, She wants to leave, I should let her leave. She can find her own way back. She has a cell phone. He thinks, she has made the decision to jump out of our car in some shitty post-industrial part of town, she's an adult, she can deal with the consequences of that decision.

Robert slows to a stop, leans over to close the passenger-side door, and takes a series of deep breaths. None of the breaths seem as deep as they should be. It's like his lungs catch at a certain point and won't go any further, just before he's finished breathing all the way in.

He circles back to find Viola.

There's a motion under a billboard, near where she ran from the car. Robert parks and opens his door and calls out to see if it's Viola. A moment later there's a loud crack that sounds exactly like how gunshots sound on television. It takes Robert a moment to realize that the sound was, in fact, a gunshot. Someone runs off into the darkness.

There is a terrible feeling in Robert's stomach. He can make out another figure underneath the billboard. It's still moving. Robert runs towards the billboard. He tells himself that it can't possibly be Viola. It isn't. "Thank God," Robert says, out of breath.

"I don't think I'm going to be okay," says the man lying on the ground.

"I'm going to call the police," Robert says. "I thought you were my wife. But I'm going to call the police."

"I don't think I'm going to be okay," the man says. "I'm not going to be okay, am I?" The man is middle-aged, white, well-dressed, with a thick white beard and fat red face. He looks like Santa Claus. He's lying on his back, clutching at his abdomen.

Robert dials 911 and gives his location. "There's a man here. I think he's been shot. I'm pretty sure he's been shot. I'm not supposed to move him, am I?"

The operator tells Robert not to move him.

"I was pretty sure I wasn't supposed to move him."

"Are you alright, sir? Are you in a safe location?"

Robert thinks about this for a moment. "Oh, God," he says, and then starts yelling for Viola.

“I’m sorry,” he says to the operator. “I have to make another call.”

Viola answers on the first ring. “What’s going on?” she asks. “Why haven’t you been answering your phone? What’s going on? Are you alright?”

“Where are you?” he says. “Can you see the car?”

ROBERT IS IN a small room at the police station. There are two police officers in the room with him, one small, squat, somehow feminine, the other quite a bit larger and vaguely Slavic looking. They keep asking if Robert would like a cup of coffee. It's nearly one and Robert is visibly shaking. He would not like a cup of coffee, not really.

"We're pretty sure you're not our guy," the more effeminate officer tells him.

"Good," Robert says. "That's good. Especially since you've already told me I'm not under any suspicion."

"For one thing, what motive could you possibly have? For another thing, what did you do with the weapon?" The officer stares at Robert as if waiting for an answer.

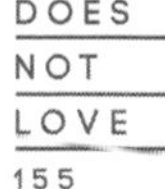

"Was that a question?" Robert says, after a moment.

The officer laughs and clasps his hands together. "Oh, you're good. You're not going to just walk into a setup like that, are you, Mr. St. Clair? He's good, Ivan."

"He said he was a lawyer, didn't he?" says the second, larger officer. "They're slippery."

"I'm not under any suspicion, right?" Robert says. "I thought I wasn't under any suspicion."

"At this stage in the process," says the first officer, "we are simply trying to establish that this shooting followed the same MO as the previous shootings. You, as an eyewitness, can help us establish that. You look like you could use a cup of coffee. Ivan, could you please get Mr. Robert St. Clair a cup of coffee?"

The second officer leaves and returns with a cup of coffee.

"Alright, so this guy you say you saw," he says, putting the coffee down in front of Robert. "Was he tall or short?"

"Tall?" Robert says, unsure.

"Like would you say six-foot-three? Six-foot-four? Six-foot-five?"

"I don't know," Robert says.

"You don't know how tall he was," the second officer says. "Man says he's seen the guy, doesn't even know how tall he was."

"There are problems of perspective to be taken into account here," says the first officer. "Depending on the angle, of course—"

"Was this guy white or black?"

"It was hard to tell, it was dark . . . "

"Doesn't even know the ethnicity! Guy's coming in here, says he can ID our perp, doesn't even know the ethnicity!"

"It was dark," Robert says. "And anyhow I never said—"

"Of course it was dark!" says the second officer. "It was night! You think we can just decide to do our job during the day? You think taxpayers would stand for that? You think, maybe, we can ask the criminal element to hold off on all illicit activities between the hours of eight pm to six am?"

"I'm sure he's not suggesting that, Ivan."

"You know what I'd like to do?" the second officer says to Robert. "I'd like to take that coffee you're drinking right now and throw it in your smug, law-school face. Would you like that? Would you like it if I threw that coffee in your smug law-school face?"

"Of course he wouldn't like that," the first officer says. "Why would you even ask such a thing?"

"In terms of noses would you say that the man you saw had more of an upturned or a downturned nose?"

"I don't know," Robert says.

"I'd like to bash your head into the wall!" the second officer screams. "Would you like that? Would you like it if I bashed your smug, law-school face into this concrete wall, right here?"

"This is harassment," Robert says. "I'm not under suspicion for committing any crime, am I?"

"Ivan has suffered a number of disappointments in his life," the first officer tells Robert, sitting in the chair beside him, putting a hand on Robert's shoulder. "Chief among them being that, coming from a family of lawyers, he was expected to follow in their footsteps. His mother went to Yale, top of the class. His father and brother both went to Brown, and didn't do so bad for themselves, either."

"I choked on the LSAT," the second officer says, as if Robert were somehow at fault for this.

"He choked on the LSAT," the first officer says with a shrug. "Of course we're all sure that he would've made an excellent lawyer, but some people just aren't good at standardized tests."

"I never choked on no test before."

"He's a hell of a detective," the first officer says. "We're glad to have him on the force, as you can imagine."

"I'd like to choke this fucking asshole," shaking a fist at Robert.

"Ivan, really, enough. We're going to have a lawsuit on our hands."

"I can't even stand looking at this guy. I need to get some air."

The second officer glares at Robert and leaves.

"He has a gruff exterior, but his heart is pure," the first officer says.

"Look, if I'm under any suspicion, I need to call my lawyer."

"Who said you were under any suspicion?"

"So I'm free to go?"

"The world is a complicated thing," says the officer, standing once again and beginning to pace, "full of many moving parts. You mentioned lawyers. You yourself are a lawyer, of course, and one of your firm's clients, we happen to know, is Obadiah Birch Pharmaceuticals. And the man who was shot? A researcher, contracted to work with Obadiah Birch Pharmaceuticals. It is entirely possible that this is a coincidence, these two things coming together, a lawyer working for Birch Pharmaceuticals and a researcher, now dead, also working for Birch Pharmaceuticals. But you must understand that these are exactly the sorts of coincidences we look for, here in the force: the coming together of two such related things. We strive to put the world in some kind of order, to turn the chaos of sensation into the beauty of theory, of explanation." He sighs pleasantly at this last phrase, a smile briefly playing across his lips; until, at the next moment, he frowns at a sudden thought, and his face bunches together, as if working it through with some difficulty.

"On the other hand—speaking of order—it stands to reason that the guy who plugged this researcher is the same guy who plugged the other researchers. And if that's so, and if just for the sake of argument you were our guy, why would you, our guy, call 911 after plugging this researcher, when our guy didn't call 911 after plugging previous researchers? Calling 911 doesn't fit our guy's MO. Unless—oh, this is the tricky part!—unless our guy's smart enough to change his MO from time to time, to throw us off the trail. You're a pretty smart guy, aren't you, Mr. St. Clair? Smart enough to change your MO, just to throw a couple of old detectives off the trail? In which case we'd have to reexamine the entire concept of MO. Meaning, in effect, reexamining the concept of causality itself. What is an MO if not an essence, the hard core underlying the varying methods of the criminal? The theme that ties act to person? The concept, in other words, of order itself?

"I see you are trembling, Mr. St. Clair. It is a terrifying idea, living in a world without order. I understand why the idea would frighten you.

"Of course, it's possible that is not the reason you are trembling. You look fatigued, Mr. St. Clair. You've had a long day. If I had had such a day, only to end up in an interrogation room in a police station, with some mincing dwarf of a police detective talking to me about MOs and causality and science, I think I might be trembling too. I would maybe want to get something off my chest. Possibly there is something you want to get off your chest, Mr. St. Clair. But not quite yet! First—yes, first, let me show you something. It is behind this door," hand in place, readying himself to open it, "something that, I think, will bring this night to—" A polite knocking comes from the other side of the door. The detective opens it, just a crack.

"Ivan!" hisses the first officer. "What the hell. Where's the other witness? How can we have the big payoff without the other witness?"

"There was another witness?" Robert asks.

"We never actually managed to pick up the other witness," comes the second officer's voice, from the other side of the door.

"Why wasn't I told about there being another witness?" Robert says, standing. His voice is reaching what sounds, even to his own ears, like an uncomfortably high pitch.

"You told me they were bringing him in," the first officer says, opening the door fully to reveal the second officer, looking sheepish. "How can we have the big payoff if they didn't bring him in?"

"They were going to," says the second officer. "And then they didn't. He disappeared."

"Disappeared?"

"Vanished, into the moonlight. They found this," he holds up a tuft of what appears to be brown fake fur. "And this," he holds up a pair of black goggles. The officers stand hunched over the interrogation table, examining the evidence.

"Look, am I free to go or aren't I?" Robert says, finally.

"Yes, dammit, yes," says the first officer. "Did anyone once say, this entire time, that you weren't free to go?"

"I'VE NEVER SEEN anyone die before," Viola tells the FBI agent. They're sitting on the bed of the FBI agent's motel room eating peanut butter crackers bought from a vending machine by the motel-room door. Viola twists each pair of crackers apart before she eats them. "You've seen people die before, right?"

"Not that I'm at liberty to divulge."

"Oh, sure, not that you're at liberty to divulge. Right." Viola twists apart a pair of peanut butter crackers and leaves them sitting peanut-butter-side-up on her lap. She thinks. She says, "I would have thought it would be terrifying, but it's more complicated than that. The man practically died in Robert's arms, and there's part of me that's, like, envious. I'm trying to figure out how to articulate it." The FBI agent sits with a patient expression on his face, while she tries to figure out how to articulate it. “It’s stupid,” Viola says. “Never mind.”

The FBI agent drives Viola to a large concrete building on the outskirts of Indianapolis. Inside the building are other men in suits like the FBI agent’s. Every time Viola and the FBI agent come to a door he punches in a code on a keypad and puts his eye in front of a scanner for a retinal scan. Each room they enter into gets colder, until Viola can see her breath. The walls of the last room are lined with drawers. The FBI agent pulls out a drawer.

“That’s not him,” Viola says.

The FBI agent pulls out another drawer.

“That’s him.”

Viola and the FBI agent both look at the body of the dead researcher. He looks like Santa Claus.

“What do I do?” Viola says.

The FBI agent shrugs. He starts to put his hand between her legs. Viola slaps his hand away.

“I mean, am I supposed to mourn him? Or am I supposed to feel some sort of, like, awe?”

“He has a family,” the FBI agent says, looking at the man’s chart. “We’re investigating the family, though we don’t suppose that will turn up anything.”

The FBI agent and Viola leave and get back in the car. On the radio an actress who had achieved success early in life talks about how it wasn’t easy on her, achieving success early in life. Viola suddenly feels sad and self-conscious. She wants to ask the FBI agent to turn the radio off, but she's worried that he will intuit how sad and self-conscious she's feeling right now. Then she asks him to turn off the radio anyway. The FBI agent says that the actress is one of his favorite actresses, but turns off the radio.

"It's like I've got a hole inside me where I should have an assurance of love," Viola says. "I look at other people going about their day, doing the kinds of things people do, shopping for groceries, driving cars, picking up and putting down objects of various sizes, and the only way I can imagine that they can keep doing all of that is that somewhere inside them they have an assurance of love. They don't even have to think about it, because they know it's there. But I think about it all the time, because it's not."

The FBI agent frowns at her.

"That doesn't make any sense," Viola says. "I don't know why I said it."

Then later, she says: "When I was first dating Robert, I used to steal things from him. Little things, things I was pretty sure he wouldn't notice: pens, a tie he never wore, one or two out of about a bazillion wine glasses he had. The way I thought about it was this: He liked me then, sure, but there was absolutely no guarantee that he was going to keep liking me in the future. But if I had things of his, I knew they weren't going anywhere."

"Do you still have them? The stuff you stole?"

"One of the wine glasses, I think. I think the other stuff got lost the last time we moved."

In the motel parking lot Viola and the FBI agent do an awkward kind of hug, and Viola goes to her car and leaves.

ROBERT CRUSHES UP a pill and stirs it into Viola's coffee, then crushes up another and stirs it into his own coffee. The next day Robert crushes up a pill for Viola's coffee, and one pill for his own coffee. It seems fairer this way. If there are any adverse unintended effects he should experience them as much as she does.

Later, he gets the idea to crush up several pills at once and mix them in with the sugar. Provided he first measures the amount of sugar in the sugar bowl, so that two spoonfuls of sugar (the amount Viola takes in her coffee) equal one pill. The crushed-up pills, white, fit in well enough with the sugar that Robert doubts even a very close inspection would alert someone to their presence. And, as Trey told him, the pills are absolutely tasteless. There is a danger, of course, that Viola might drink more than one cup of coffee in the morning while at home. But she rarely does this. Rarely, enough, for it to be a negligible concern? Robert resolves that if Viola does drink a second cup of coffee at home, Robert will drink a second cup as well.

THERE IS a very difficult winter.

ROBERT RECEIVES A LETTER in the mail. The return address reads REDACTED. Robert takes the letter to his office and sits for some time with the letter before him on his desk. He feels the presentiment of a terrible guilt. He opens it, finally, with trembling hands. "Robert St. Clair," the letter begins,

"Previously we would have assembled the text of this letter from words cut and pasted from magazines. It was our habit to do so, in cases similar to yours, long after the advent of the laser printer and its corresponding increase in the possibilities of anonymity. Partly, we liked the air of menace thereby created in the mind of the reader. Partly, we just liked the tradition of the thing. More than either of these reasons, however, we were attached to the way that the cut-and-paste letter allowed a new message, our message, to emerge from others' words. Even now, although we have changed our technology of choice, the method remains the same: each word of this letter has been taken from some other text. This letter, and its message, existed long before human hands digitally cut and pasted it into the form you now see.

"Our voice is the voice of the people, Robert. The law we represent is an emergent law.

"We have seen what you are doing, Robert. We have observed you. We do not need to tell you what you will be charged with—are charged with, Robert, for the charges have already been filed, invisibly, and the court sits in invisible judgment. You know your guilt—and, as we are the court of the invisible, it is ultimately your knowledge, and not your actions, that must be judged."

Robert hides the letter in the emptiness behind the bathroom sink. More letters arrive, daily, a series of terrible, unspecified threats. For some reason, the idea of Viola finding one of these letters fills him with dread—as though she would know, already, what he was guilty of.

ROBERT KEEPS A LIST of potential unintended adverse effects that he has experienced, or that he has noticed Viola exhibiting, since he began adding the drug that Trey gave him to their coffee each morning:

nervousness
fear of discovery
moodiness, irritability (Viola)
sudden spiraling moments of hopelessness
distraction
guilt
boredom (Viola)
lack of professional motivation
hours spent looking at vacation destinations on the internet, or clicking on links for additional information about topics I don't care about (celebrities, celebrities' children, celebrities' pregnancies, plane crashes)

sweating (noticeable)
difficulty sleeping
sleeping too much
difficulty dreaming, or difficulty in dreams
directionless anger
emptiness
emptiness
emptiness

ROBERT AND HIS FRIEND Trey get after-work drinks at the Slippery Noodle, the oldest jazz bar in Indianapolis. "Hey," Trey says, gesturing towards the band. "Whaddayaknow? It's our old friends." Antonio waves at them from the stage. Hugo nods in their direction while performing an excellent solo on his trombone.

"Didn't know you boys played jazz," Trey says, between sets.

"They pay pretty well at these gigs," Antonio says. "And it's a little more dignified, I suppose, if you go for that sort of thing."

"Dignity?" says Trey. "I'm a salesman, and my buddy here? A lawyer. Robert. Robert! What kind of law do you practice, Robert?"

"Corporate litigation," Robert says, who's already slightly drunker than he meant to be.

"Corporate litigation, woo," says Antonio, shaking his head. "Well, we're going to be at the Black Box after hours, if you fellows are interested."

"Of course we are," says Trey.

"I think I'd better head home," says Robert.

"Robert, buddy, you are in no condition to drive," Trey says, clapping him on the shoulder. Then, turning back to Antonio, "What's the address? I'll put it into my phone."

"No address," Antonio says, and draws him a map on a napkin.

The Black Box social club and bar turns out to be behind a façade painted entirely black, not far from the Greyhound station. A bouncer shines a light in Trey and Robert's eyes before letting them enter. Inside, the walls are lined with pictures of planes in downward spirals or crumpled and smoking after a crash. Antonio and Hugo are at a low table in the corner, drinking something called a Hull Loss, the ingredients of which the bar's owner has spent his career refusing to divulge even to the local authorities. The musicians have already bought a round for Trey and Robert. "I'm driving," Trey insists. "You'll have to give mine to Robert here."

The owner of the bar, whom Antonio says is a friend of his family from back in California, was a commercial pilot for twenty-some years. He settled down after he miraculously survived a mid-air crash over Indiana during the air traffic controllers' strike in the eighties.

Robert finishes his Hull Loss. Trey has disappeared. People are dancing. A woman in a too-short orange dress is dancing right by Robert's chair, bumping him with her hip. He keeps pushing her away. He feels terrible. He tries to explain to Hugo and Antonio about the difficulty of trying to determine whether his wife is once again beginning to love him. "She did love me, once," Robert says. "I think that just . . . it was a lot to deal with. For both of us. My friend Trey thinks it's treatable. Her condition."

"What is her condition?"

"That she doesn't love me anymore."

Hugo looks at Robert with concern. Antonio stares at the woman in the short orange dress, who is once more bumping Robert with her hip.

"I MET HER at a party in Ann Arbor," drunken Robert tells Hugo and Antonio, as the Black Box slowly fills around them. "It was a mixer that one of my housemates was throwing, with the express purpose of giving humanities students an opportunity to hook up with law students. My housemates were horrible people. One of Viola's friends dragged her to it because she thought it would be hilarious. I think that Viola's friend might have been a slightly horrible person, too. The friend left early, but Viola stayed, talking to me. She had mistaken me, at first, for another humanities student, and asked how I'd ended up there. I wasn't dressed like a lawyer, she said. How do lawyers dress, I asked. She gestured around the room. 'Kind of like assholes?' she said. I laughed.

"I remember she was wearing these earrings, they looked a little like black pearls. They were trilobites, she said, fossils. 'Actual fossils?' I said. 'Yeah,' she said. It turns out actual fossils aren't that rare, anybody can just go and buy them in a rocks shop. That floored me, that there are so many fossils in the world that somebody could just go and make earrings out of them.

"I think that we met at the exact right time, for both of us. I had just finished sowing my oats. I'd never expected that I would do much sowing of oats, when I was younger—I viewed myself, even as a child, as steadier than that; the idea of 'wild years' always seemed like something other people experienced—but then in my mid-twenties, much to my surprise, I had them. A series of wild years. I couldn't get on the bus or walk down the street in Ann Arbor without longing. I dated several women during this period who I did not love, and had no intention of loving. I once or twice went out to a bar and bought women drinks and flashed money around, much to my present embarrassment. And then, just as suddenly as they had appeared, my wild years left. I found myself, at the age of twenty-six, ready to settle down, with no one in mind to settle down with. And then I met Viola.

"She had been through a string of terrible relationships herself, with men who were worthless. Some of these men, I think, were physically violent. She told me that for a long time, she had no particular intentions of settling down, ever. For example, for most of her life she'd assumed that she wouldn't ever want kids. But she got burned by too many men.

"Perhaps I was too ready to see myself as an endpoint. To see her life as leading inevitably to me. I would be steady, for her, and we would settle down and be happy. I took the Indiana Bar and we moved here, to Indianapolis, and we fit ourselves into a certain narrative. Except then it didn't happen. She experienced miscarriage after miscarriage, with no explanation. And it was like we woke up from something. It was like we had been watching a movie, and all of a sudden the house lights had come up, and ushers had descended upon us, with terrible looks that asked what we thought we were doing, still in our seats."

TREY RETURNS to the table with another round. "See that little black box in the corner over there? There's a guy at the bar, says you can put your ear up to the earpiece connected to it and you'll hear the last five seconds of your life."

"I have tried it once," says Hugo, nodding.

"And? Did you hear the last five seconds of your life?"

Hugo shrugs. "Hard to know. It is very possible."

"I don't know if I would want to hear that," says Robert.

"You're a bunch of suckers," Trey says. "It's a joke. Of course it's a joke."

"So are you going to try it out?" Robert asks.

"I don't need to try it out. It's a joke."

Hugo and Antonio talk about different types of guitar. Trey seems lost in thought. After a moment, he says, "Look, I'll prove it's a joke," and walks over to the black box and puts the earpiece to his ear. Several minutes later he comes back to the table, visibly shaken. "It was my own voice," he says. "It was my own voice, just like it sounds in my head."

"What'd it say?" Robert asks. But Trey doesn't want to talk about it.

HUGO TELLS ROBERT and Trey about the leader of the guinea-piggers, Jeremy, who came from a good family but fell into guinea-pigging after some financial difficulties. "He lives on the outskirts of town," Hugo says. "In a storage facility purchased many years ago by Obadiah Birch Pharmaceuticals, and used as temporary housing for long-term guinea-piggers."

"That facility was shut down years ago," Trey says.

"Guinea-piggers?" Robert asks.

"Volunteer human test subjects," Trey clarifies.

"Every few years there is a raid," Hugo says. "The men in riot gear show up to force the guinea-piggers out of the storage facility by court order, and they are taken to hospital psych wards, or simply dropped off on the outskirts of town. But soon they return. Many have no other place to go. Many are illegal residents, or have bad credit, or feel as though they have found a community among the guinea-piggers."

"What you're talking about—if it existed—would be illegal," Trey says; then, to Robert, "The facility was shut down years ago. It would be trespassing. The state of Indiana would be well within their rights to force these people to leave the area."

"A single bus line runs by the storage facility," Hugo continues. "Other than that, the only vehicles that approach are the white vans of the researchers, who arrive with their lists and call out: Male, in good health, 18 to 24. Female, in good health, 35 to 40. Male, in good health, 33 to 45."

"In good health?" Antonio asks.

"It's a phase I study," Trey says. "In a phase I study you're testing the safety of a drug, rather than its efficacy. Phase I studies start with healthy volunteers. Phase II studies are the ones that target people who actually have the condition you're trying to treat."

"You take the drug, and they see if it does anything terrible to you, and then they give you some money," Hugo says.

"An honorarium," Trey explains. "By law, all participants in a phase I study have to be healthy volunteers. You don't pay volunteers. But it is reasonable to recompense them for their time. If you didn't recompense them for their time, you wouldn't have any healthy volunteers for your phase I studies."

Hugo frowns. "Many of the guinea-piggers are not in good health. Many have not recovered from previous phase I studies."

"Then they shouldn't be volunteering," Trey says. "They shouldn't be signing forms that *specifically* say that they are in good health." Then, turning again to Robert, "I mean, are we supposed to assume that our volunteers are lying to us?"

Robert looks down at his drink, concerned.

"That's assuming, for the sake of argument, that any of this is happening. This fairy tale." Trey gestures at Hugo. "I mean, who is this guy? Some trombone player. Some asshole making a few bucks on the side from pharmaceutical trials."

"Hey," Antonio says, starting to stand up.

Hugo motions for him to sit down. He takes a moment to gather his thoughts, then continues speaking, in the same calm, sad voice. "Jeremy, the leader of the guinea-piggers, is a good man. He is trying to organize the guinea-piggers, to have a voice in the conditions of their labor."

Trey snorts. "For God's sake."

"But there are other, darker forces at work. Guinea-piggers who strive toward violent revolution, who want to take revenge not only on the pharmaceutical companies, but on the city itself. Rumors of a man in black goggles and a fake fur coat who carries two pistols, and stalks the night for researchers who have been sloppy in their phase I testing. Some say that he is exacting vengeance for the death of his son, or perhaps his wife; others, that he himself was killed as the result of a phase I study gone wrong, and it is his spirit who is carrying out these murderous deeds . . . "

IT'S FOUR A.M. by the time Robert gets home. Viola is not in bed. He wakes up several hours later, still wearing his clothes from the night before, minus his suit jacket. He gets up and wanders the house, trying to find the jacket. All around him he hears voices, a messy, conflicting jangle. His head feels thick, part hungover, part still drunk. These voices, he thinks. Is this an unintended adverse effect? Eventually he realizes that the television is on. He turns it off. The radio is on. He turns that off, too. He goes from room to room, turning off televisions and radios. I don't remember turning any of this on last night, he thinks. Perhaps Viola did it. Perhaps she came home at some point while I was sleeping and turned on every television and radio in the house. Why would she do that, he thinks. Could that be an unintended adverse effect, the need to be surrounded by voices? To be blanketed by them? He can see how, in a certain way, it would be comforting. He tries to think back to the unintended adverse effects that Trey listed for him. He cannot remember if "needing to be blanketed by voices," or some corresponding scientific term, was on the list.

He finds the suit jacket several days later, at the bottom of a pile of laundry. In the jacket pocket is a note from Hugo, with a phone number on it. Robert calls the number. "Robert," Hugo says. "I am glad you decided to call. We think that you could be very useful to us."

AT THE LIBRARY no one talks about the FBI agent anymore. He is still there, but no one seems willing to indicate that they so much as notice him. It is as though he has become a shared secret. Has he issued National Security Letters to other librarians, Viola wonders. Who else is he fucking?

VIOLA STANDS OUTSIDE waiting for the FBI agent in a floral-print sundress with a halter-style top that someone once told her was flattering on her, but then she gets cold and decides that he's probably not actually going to come and goes inside and puts on a sweater. Five minutes later her cell phone buzzes. The FBI agent asks why she isn't outside. Viola goes outside and gets into the FBI agent's car.

This is the sweater with the oil stain on it, Viola thinks. I always forget that about this sweater. I guess I keep hoping that it will come out in the wash, but it never does. It's not noticeable, though, she thinks. Or I don't think it is. Only a little darker than the rest of the sweater, but it's a dark sweater to begin with. It's weird how I don't ever really notice my body or my clothes when I'm by myself. Like I can have dirt and crap all over my skirt and not notice until somebody else comes into the room. And then I can't *not* notice. Viola sits with her hands under her legs, thinking about the oil stain on her sweater, telling herself that it's not noticeable.

The FBI agent asks how her day was. "It was fine," she says. "A little boring. I caught a kid stealing some books in the Children's Section but then he got away before me or Jeanette could catch him."

"What did he look like?"

"The kid? He looked like a kid."

"It could be important, what he looked like. Did he have little things on his head?"

"Little things?"

"Like horns."

"Why would he be wearing horns?"

"It was just a question."

Sometimes Viola likes to think that because of the NSL nobody else can actually see the FBI agent when she's with him. She imagines the drivers of cars they pass reacting in horror at seeing her riding in a car that drives itself. She imagines the other drivers so surprised that they crash into railings and trees and other cars behind the FBI agent's car. Viola sits beside the FBI agent picturing constant car crashes in their wake.

They stop at a storage facility on the far west

side. The FBI agent pulls a cloth tote bag from the backseat and steps out of the car. "Stick close to me," he tells her. She wants to mock him: *stick close to me*, serious, eyes slitted, but she doesn't.

Smoke rises from the storage facility. There are little bonfires all over the place. For a moment Viola imagines that the storage facility has been carpet-bombed, pictures planes flying low. Then she notices people tending the fires. The people tending the fires are staring at Viola and the FBI agent. "Don't say anything," the FBI agent says, putting on a pair of sunglasses. "Just walk. Act like you own the place. Keep in mind that they're more scared of you than you are of them." Viola wonders if the FBI agent is going to flash his gun at anybody.

They walk into a storage unit near the periphery. A man looks up from a battery-powered, handheld television set and smiles as they enter. "Good evening, Agent. Business or pleasure?"

"Don't be cute," says the FBI agent.

The man pushes away the carpet that had been under his feet, and then pulls open the trapdoor that had been under the carpet. Viola follows the FBI agent down a metal staircase. The room beneath is filled with bins of VHS tapes, each of them, so far as Viola can tell, labeled in the same manner as the tapes she found in the FBI agent's suitcase. Men, some dressed in suits like the FBI agent's, others in uniform, scour the bins, shuffling through the videos, examining each of the labels. This is the black market, Viola thinks. The guy who let us down here, he was probably a member of the mafia or some other criminal organization. I suppose they exist everywhere. They serve a useful function in society. All of the other men in here, they're part of the official power structure, but they still need the mafia in order to pass these videos back and forth. Viola thinks about stealing one of the FBI agent's videos when she goes back to the motel room in Danville, sometime when his back is turned, just out of curiosity. But does she really want to see a video of the girl some two-star general's fucking? It's not really her thing, she decides. Though she doesn't have a problem with it, in the abstract. She thinks about the two-star general watching a video of her. She wonders if anyone in here has already seen a video of her. She tries to catch their eyes. Nothing.

After a little while Viola follows the FBI agent back upstairs and out the trapdoor.

"Tell me if you see anyone you recognize," the FBI agent says, on the way back to the car.

"Why would I recognize anyone?"

"It was just a question." They get back into the car and Viola gives the FBI agent a long look. "Don't look at me like that," he says, and they drive off.

VIOLA AND THE FBI agent have dinner at a sushi restaurant on the near west side. The FBI agent is saying goodbye to a friend of his, a white-haired but healthy older gentleman who is retiring from his post as judge. He had presided for more than a decade over one of the most prestigious of the secret courts.

"Many people believe that today's secret courts, the ones that deal with Terror, are the only secret courts there have ever been," he says. "But there are other courts, much older, much more secret, that deal with, for example, matters of the heart."

"Like what?" Viola asks.

"Well I can't go into any detail, really," the judge says.

They order a round of plum wine. It's stronger than Viola was expecting. They order another. Music is playing in the background, a cover of "Volare" using traditional Japanese instruments. The judge recognizes the band. He's been interested in their work for some time, and he talks about it, a little.

"I don't really like music anymore," Viola says. "All of the music I used to like has too many feelings attached to it." She looks down at her nigiri and worries that that was a stupid thing to say. She worries that the white-haired judge will think she's a sad sack. After a moment she says, to clarify, "Not necessarily bad feelings." The judge nods at this, and Viola suddenly gets the idea that he's very understanding about how people can be overwhelmed, listening to music they used to like. Perhaps he's just very understanding in general. Viola looks at his hands. He has very sensitive, wise-looking hands. The FBI agent's hands look sensitive, but they don't look wise. They look something like a little boy's hands. The judge's hands are broader, more masculine, with red knuckles and wiry silver hairs. They make her think of the protagonist's friend in *Crime and Punishment*, who was big but very understanding of others; she can't remember his name, just now.

"What do you plan to do once you retire?" Viola says.

"I am retiring to study the secret body of case law," the judge says. "The secret courts operate on a hierarchy of secrecy," he explains. "For most of my career, I thought that I was presiding over the most secret court. Each court believes that, that it's the most secret. Which is absurd, of course. There's always a more secret court. I know that now."

"Always?" Viola asks.

"Theoretically." Viola wonders how he could know this, if he was on a secret court himself. Is there some absolute position from which each of the secret courts might be viewed, and to which each of the secret courts would be relative? Viola asks the judge about his family.

"They're doing very well, thank you."

"Are you looking forward to spending more time with them?"

The FBI agent and the judge talk about certain aspects of the secret body of case law. "A particularly interesting case is when a court at one level of secrecy learns of the existence of a court at a higher level of secrecy," the judge says. "Such cases function, mathematically, you might say, to create a series of imaginary or 'shadow' courts. Say for instance that court *d* learns of the existence of court *c*, which until that point had been operating at a higher level of secrecy. The court that had been court *d*, then, is no longer court *d*, rather now it is some other court, operating at a higher level of secrecy than court *c*. Call it court *b*. So court *b* now knows about court *c*, and court *c* still knows about court *d*. But what does court *c* know if it knows court *d*? It knows about a court which no longer exists—a court which is like court *b* in every respect except for one (and that one is precisely the most crucial): court *b* is a level of secrecy above court *c*, court *d* is not. Court *d* is therefore a shadow court, cast by court *b*. Each of them operates at its own level of secrecy within the hierarchy, and though their actions, to an outside observer—say, court *a*—appear the same in all respects, the meanings of those actions are radically different."

The judge draws a diagram on a napkin:

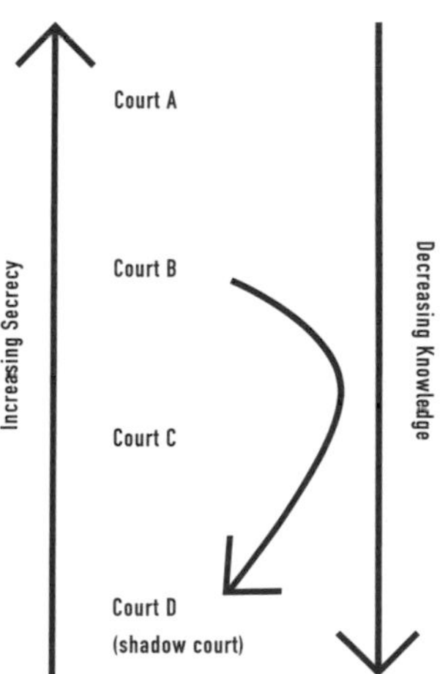

"Ultimately, the law is pure form, devoid of content," the judge tells the FBI agent. "What we are fighting for is not a thing, but a shape."

A little later, the judge says: "My wife has not been very understanding. We've had some problems. We had two kids, boys, but neither of them lives in Indiana anymore. I think one of them moved to Seattle? He was a designer. Web designer. We're not really in touch anymore. I think they both secretly call my wife, that they stay in touch with her and tell her about their lives and so forth. She won't talk to me about it."

"That sounds horrible," Viola says, putting her hand on his hand.

"She says I lost my chance with them a long time ago," the judge says. Viola notices the FBI agent staring at her hand on the judge's hand.

"Listen to me," the judge says. "Going on like this. We're celebrating, aren't we?"

The judge orders a round of sake on the rocks for the table. "A thing a lot of people don't realize about sake is that it's a very versatile drink," he says. The FBI agent and Viola and the judge toast to the judge's future, and then they toast to the FBI agent's future and Viola's future. "You kids," the judge says. "You fucking kids." The judge orders another round for the three of them and gets his money out and puts it on the table.

"You're not paying for this," the FBI agent says. "We're taking you out, remember?"

"I'm paying for whatever the hell I want to," the judge says. "It's my money and I want to spend it." He toasts again to Viola and the FBI agent. "You fucking kids," he says. "I bet you kids have some kind of fun together, don't you?" The judge is holding Viola's hand in both of his.

"We should drive him home," Viola says to the FBI agent, a little while later. "He's in no condition."

"I'm staying at a hotel," the judge says.

"Which hotel?" He tells them.

Viola and the judge follow the FBI agent out to the FBI agent's car. The judge walks with Viola's arm in his. He pats her arm. He keeps saying what a wonderful night he is having and how lovely it has been to meet her. "Put him in the front," the FBI agent says.

"That's not very gentlemanly," the judge says, but allows Viola to help him into the front seat anyhow.

At the hotel the FBI agent parks and they stand before the sliding glass doors to the hotel lobby while the judge says goodnight.

"Do you mind seeing an older gentleman up to his room?" the judge says. Viola looks at the FBI agent.

"Sure, see him up," the FBI agent says. "Do whatever the hell you're going to."

In the hotel room, which is much nicer than the room that the FBI agent is staying in, the judge respectfully embraces Viola. Viola nuzzles into the judge's neck. He's in very good shape. She can feel how good of shape he's in, in the muscles in the arms with which the judge is respectfully and gently embracing her. She asks the judge how often he takes young women up to hotel rooms with him.

"I enjoy the occasional guest," the judge says. "I try to be appropriate, you know."

"Very appropriate," Viola says. "I'd imagine."

The judge can't get a hardon. It's only half-there. He's very pleasant about it. "Other men I've been with aren't so, you know, accepting when that happens."

"I'm seventy-six years old," the judge says, "and I'm in a hotel room with a beautiful young woman. I'm having a wonderful time in any case. My only concern is that you not think it's any commentary on you."

"Oh, no," Viola says. "But I appreciate your concern."

They sit on the hotel-room bed, the judge in his boxers, Viola readjusting her skirt. "You can spend the night," the judge says. "I never kick my guests out. Never. It's out of the question."

"I can get a taxi," Viola says. "Really, it's fine. You've been quite the gentleman."

The FBI agent is still waiting outside the hotel doors when Viola comes back down. Viola realizes, as soon as she sees him, that she's actually not at all surprised that he waited.

"You're jealous," she says.

"Why shouldn't I be jealous?" he says.

"Look, this is an affair," Viola says, getting in the car. "I have a husband."

"You don't love him."

The FBI agent drives through the city towards the motel, where Viola's car is parked. Viola asks for a cigarette, mostly to break the silence.

"I have proof that you don't love him," the FBI agent says. "Photographs, video and audio recordings."

"Jesus."

"And that *he doesn't love you*."

Viola stares out the window at a series of abandoned factories passing by. "He loves me," she says.

"He doesn't deserve you."

"He loves me," Viola says. "I don't want to hear you say that he doesn't love me again. Because it's not true."

VIOLA BRUSHES her teeth in the empty house feeling very alone. She tries to think about her situation with the FBI agent and with Robert and about what effect going up to his hotel room with the judge might have had on the situation, but none of her thoughts come in words. She pictures herself asleep under a snow drift, curled up. It doesn't seem sad or self-pitying to her. It's just a very comfortable picture. But of course it's too late in the year for snow. As she's brushing her teeth she lists places in her head where it would still be snowing this time of year. Alaska. Some place in Canada. Michigan, Upper Peninsula. Certain mountaintops in Chile or Argentina. She makes a big production out of smoothing out the bed sheets and turning back the covers. Robert isn't home yet. Robert doesn't come back all night. She lies under the covers, staring at the ceiling, until early in the morning, thinking.

VIOLA MEETS the retired judge for brunch at a restaurant near the river walk downtown. After brunch they take a walk along the river. As they walk the judge holds Viola's arm and asks about her upbringing in the South.

"You don't have an accent," he says.

"People always tell me that, but it's not true. I have a Raleigh accent. This is what people from Raleigh sound like."

"Perhaps you've been in the Midwest too long," the judge says. "We don't have accents either."

The judge has brought along a couple of paper cups and a thermos of rosé and chipped ice. They find a bench facing the water and he pours a cup for Viola and one for himself. "This is lovely," he says. "Soon the weather will get too hot for this to be so comfortable."

They talk about the river walk, and the recently announced plans for its expansion. Viola thinks, I'm glad that we didn't have sex that night. There was a moment, of course . . . And he is in remarkably good shape . . . But he's kind of a father figure. I like that, that he's just a father figure. It's much less complicated between us if he's a father figure and we didn't have sex. Viola had a friend in her MLS program who had a thing for father figures. This friend was very proud of it, or proud enough to tell Viola and some other people, anyway. She only dated men who were older, and who looked more or less like her dad. Viola wonders what happened to her. Then she remembers: she married someone at Robert's firm. That's funny that I would have forgotten about that, she thinks.

The judge pours them each another cupful of rosé. "What should we toast to?"

"We forgot to toast last time," Viola says.

"That's why it's so important that we toast this time."

"I don't want to toast to anything important," Viola says. "Let's toast to chipped ice."

"Chipped ice is very important," the judge says, but they toast to chipped ice anyhow.

A little while later Viola says, "Are you drunk?"

"I'm slightly inebriated. 'Tipsy.'" He says it in a

way that makes "tipsy" sound like it's something only other people say.

"'Tipsy,'" Viola says, saying it the same way, smiling. "'Tipsy.' Isn't this illegal, drinking out in the open? Aren't you supposed to uphold the law?"

"I'm only sworn to uphold the secret law. And I'm retired."

"Am I breaking any secret laws?"

"If you were I couldn't tell you."

"I feel like that's all I ever hear, recently. For once in my life, I'd like to know what I'm doing wrong."

"*If* you're doing anything wrong," the judge says. Viola glowers at him. "You seem to have gotten very serious all of a sudden," he says, dividing the last of the thermos between their cups.

"I'm not sad," Viola says.

"No one accused you of being sad."

"Oh. I thought maybe you did."

Viola and the judge observe couples paddling by in paddle-boats. They drink the last of the rosé. Viola sits fiddling with her cup.

"Here," the judge says. "Let me show you something." He peels back a place in his skin, an area perhaps an inch square on his forearm. Viola peers into the area that he has peeled away.

"What do you see?"

"Nothing," she says.

"After so many years, I have started to become the law myself," he says. "A kind of structured emptiness."

"Am I allowed to see that?" Viola asks.

"Anyone is," he says. "There's nothing there to see. That is how the law remains secret: it isn't there." The judge replaces the flap of skin that he had peeled and pats it down.

Viola makes a small basket out of grass while they're sitting on the bench and hands it to the judge.

"Where did you learn to do that?"

"I've just always known."

"It's lovely."

"Thank you," Viola says. She makes another. "When I close my eyes and think about the last several months, I picture a whirlpool, or a tornado. A ring of violence circling and circling around nothing. Continually drawling everything towards that emptiness in the center."

"I see," the judge says.

"I wanted to be a nun when I was younger, have I told you that?" Viola says. "Or a saint."

"I didn't realize you were Catholic."

"I'm not."

The judge examines the basket, holding it gently up to the light.

“Maybe secretly you thought I was sad,” Viola says, as they're walking back to their cars. “But you didn't want to tell me, because you saw how serious I'd gotten. You didn't want to ruin our good time.”

“You're a charming young woman,” the judge says, as they're standing by her car.

“I can't tell if you're being serious.”

“I'm absolutely being serious.”

“I thought you were,” Viola says. “But you can see why it was important for me to make sure. I had a good day.” The judge gives her a peck on the cheek.

“I'm glad we didn't have sex that time, when I took you to your room,” Viola says. The judge looks at her, dejected. She tries to explain about how she likes him better as a father figure, and he says that he understands, but she's pretty sure he doesn't. “It was a compliment,” Viola says.

“I understand,” the judge says. He kisses her check again, but it's not the same.

Viola gets in her car and says to herself, stupid. She watches the judge walk back to his car in her rearview mirror. He is still holding the tiny grass basket. She thinks, why do I always have to explain myself about everything? Why can't I just let something be? Viola thinks, I should get out of my car and go after him. She thinks, anything I do now would make him feel worse. She thinks, if I were him, wouldn't I want me just to disappear right now, so I'd never have to think about me again?

VIOLA DISAPPEARS. There is a Viola-shaped hole in reality, where Viola used to be. The Viola-shaped hole in reality sits with the FBI agent in the motel room and watches videos that he has taken in which he pretends to interrogate her. Except, she thinks, I haven't seen this video before. That's not even me. The image quality is bad: horizontal white lines wash up and down the screen like waves. Is it possible that we are watching an actual interrogation? Is there a market for interrogations, passed back and forth between members of the intelligence community, the government, police forces, amateur enthusiasts, connoisseurs? It is not the content of the interrogation that is important, she thinks, but the form . . . If you hurt someone enough, scare them enough, they will say whatever you want them to. It is a way of turning someone else's body into a kind of puppet. Content becomes meaningless: you may as well be talking to yourself. But the form, the ritual . . . A tornado, a whirlpool, violence swirling around emptiness. Love, too: a kind of violence, drawing everything into the emptiness at its center . . . Eye, she thinks. That's the term for it, the center of a tornado, that kernel of nothing. The eye.

"I want you to tell me exactly what I am allowed to do," the FBI agent says. She is lying still mostly-dressed in bed, with the FBI agent looming over her.

"What do you want to do?" she asks.

"I want you to tell me."

"Do you want to slap me?"

The FBI agent slaps her.

"Do you want to spit on me?"

The FBI agent spits on her.

When I was younger, she thinks, I wanted to live a life that was not just for myself. I wanted to do something large, something important, something pure and full of grace. When did life become such a small thing? When did I become an animal that mostly reacts? Oh yes, I loved men before Robert, and I was hurt by them, and I found Robert and decided that he would not hurt me. This is how life becomes small: you grow up, which is to say, you get hurt, and then you adjust your life in ways in which you hope you will no longer get hurt. But of course you get hurt again, and what difference does it make, who's responsible?

"I feel so bad, so much of the time," the FBI agent says. She rubs her hand through his hair.

"It's okay," she says, shushing him. "It's okay."

Somewhere, I am being watched, she thinks. On other screens. Images of me, scattered throughout the nation. She considers the FBI agent. This is not his fault, she thinks. Or not entirely. I was in the process of becoming a certain type of image—fitting a certain role—long before. Can I say that it is Robert's fault? No, not entirely—I had as much to do with it as anyone—

Robert, who was once her husband, which is to say, who was once married to an image of her, calls, over and over again, on her cell phone. She can never quite convince herself to answer it.

HUGO TAKES ROBERT to the guinea-pigger camp, which lies on the far western edge of the city. They take the bus from downtown, because Hugo is concerned that Robert's newish, expensive-looking car might attract suspicion. "What kind of suspicion?" Robert wants to know.

"They might think that we are with the mafia."

Beyond the complex's gates, rows of bright orange roll-up doors stretch off into the distance. Small fires are everywhere. Guinea-piggers look up at Robert, sweating, shaking, their eyes glazed over, many of them not seeing him as he walks past, or, if they do see him, not knowing whether he is an hallucination. Others don't even bother to look up, but continue feeding their fires with pieces of junk mail or gathered sticks. Huge flakes of ash float through the air like terrifying moths.

"This is horrible," Robert says.

"This is the underside of the world," Hugo proclaims, voice suddenly taking on dramatic-movie tones. "This is—oh, hi kids."

A group of a half-dozen kids runs by, throwing pieces of rubble at each other. One of them throws a piece of rubble at Robert, which hits him, hard, in the shoulder.

"Hey!" Hugo says. "Don't throw rubble at Robert. Robert doesn't even know how to play the rubble game."

Robert rubs his shoulder. "Did those kids have horns?"

"Horns?" Hugo asks. "Oh. The bony protrusions. Yes, certain of the younger children here have bony protrusions. It was a statistically insignificant birth defect resulting from a previous phase I drug trial that their parents participated in."

"That seemed like a lot of kids with horns that just ran by."

Hugo shrugs. "Statistics," he says.

Hugo brings Robert to Jeremy, the leader of the guinea-piggers. Jeremy is a thin, haunted-looking man, with dark circles under his eyes and a sharp face. He's the only other person in the storage facility that Robert has seen wearing a suit, though Jeremy's is in bad shape, shabby and worn through in places, with a noticeable stain near the left breast. His office is in a double-wide storage unit filled with stacks and stacks of papers. "I'm sure that Hugo has told you what I expect in return," Jeremy says.

Robert hands over the organizational chart for Obadiah Birch Pharmaceuticals. "I'm risking my neck on this," Robert says. "If it came out that I did something that went against a client's interests—"

Jeremy makes calming shushing noises. "This?" he says. "It's like I've never seen you. Oh," he says, looking with surprise at the document in his hands. "Where did this come from?"

Jeremy hands him in return a file containing information on the drug that Robert has been secretly giving his wife. "Now that we're done here," Jeremy says, "I just wanted to let you know that I despise you. As far as I'm concerned, you stand for the worst of humanity. Hugo, show this man the door."

Hugo shrugs and gestures towards the door. "Do you think you can find your way back alright?" Hugo asks.

"I think so," Robert says.

At the bus stop, Robert runs into the same gang of children. He would guess, from looking at them, that most of them are around seven or eight years old. "Are you from the mafia?" they ask.

Robert laughs. "No," he says.

"Are you from the government?"

"Nope," he says, smiling.

One of the children shoves him while two others go for his legs. Robert hits the ground, hard, and the children swarm him. "Hey!" Robert yells. One grabs his wallet. Another gets his phone. A third kid kicks him repeatedly in the kidneys. Then, just as suddenly, it's over. The bus pulls up and the kids run off before he's even had the chance to get back to his feet. Robert grabs up, as best he can, the papers that have come loose from the file folder Jeremy gave him.

"You getting on?" the bus driver calls from the open bus door.

"Did you see that?" Robert asks.

"Last bus of the day," the bus driver says.

Robert gets on but doesn't have any money for the fare. "They just took my wallet," he tries to explain. The bus driver looks at him, blankly. "Look, if you just take me to a bank," he starts.

"This ain't a taxi," the driver says.

Robert turns to the other passengers. They stare at him flatly, refusing to help.

THE SELF-STORAGE FACILITY is a kind of labyrinth, with hundreds of possible centers. There is no way to orient oneself, once one is out of sight of the metal gates—the rows of doors stretch on seemingly forever—above the doors are numbers, but it is impossible, at a glance, to understand their organization. Behind any one of these, perhaps, might wait the minotaur, in black goggles and fake fur coat, two shining pistols—Is it better to keep wandering through the labyrinth, or try to walk home? It is almost dusk—the sky is the color of sunburnt skin—both options raise, in Robert's mind, the face of the dead man, fat and red and expiring, running out of breath . . .

They didn't take my car keys, Robert thinks. If worse comes to worse, I can walk back to town—it's what, five or six miles—that's entirely possible—Still, he doesn't like the thought of walking so far through the west side at night. He keeps thinking about the dead man's red face . . . He is aware of people all around him, human bodies—for the most part, they do not pay attention to him—he is just another body—From time to time, a pair of glassy eyes takes in his suit, Robert can tell that there is an act of appraisal going on—He thinks, It is vital to look like I know where I am going. But of course he doesn't.

Robert finds a place to settle down for a moment, his back against one of the buildings' cinderblock walls, ass on cold concrete. He looks through the folder that Jeremy gave him. The pills he has been feeding to Viola and himself are being marketed under the commercial name *Milamor*, but they have previously appeared under different names—*Ligatal*, *Amebgyn*, *Keratexx*, *Sartrex*, *Cryptogest*. The true name, the pill's chemical formulation, is longer and more complex than Robert can pronounce, but its letters seem to hold a power over him, nonetheless. Previous versions, in some cases with formulation and dosage slightly tweaked, have been marketed for military purposes, for the questioning of unwilling sources, a means of instilling trust between interrogator and interrogated . . .

Glancing up, he sees a woman who looks very much like Viola. He almost calls out to her, then stops himself. Idiot, he thinks. Of course it's not her. But her face, her build is so similar—it could be her sister, or Viola in five years' time. With her is a boy maybe six years old, wearing a knit cap that doesn't entirely cover his sandy blond hair. Possibly one of the children who attacked me, Robert thinks. As if in response to this, the kid starts to turn. Robert scrambles around a corner, then peers back out.

He follows the two of them back to their storage unit, keeping as much distance as he can while maintaining a sightline. He has a sense, though, that even if the woman were to see him, she'd look right through him—as though he and this woman inhabited different planes, touching precariously at a single point. If we'd had a child when we first tried, Robert thinks, he might be this age. That could easily be his face. In the storage unit, the door still rolled up to let in the air, the woman takes off the boy's cap and, crouching down, rubs at his cheeks and nose with a wet-nap. With the cap gone, Robert can see, even from this distance, two horns, or boney protrusions, one above each eye. Robert is filled with sympathy. There is so much suffering in the world, he thinks. Why are we made like this, that we can only feel someone else's suffering when we can imagine it to be our own? I will become a benefactor, Robert thinks. I will raise up this people from their suffering.

The woman lights a kerosene stove and uses it to heat the contents of two cans of food, which she then spoons onto a pair of plates. The boy eats ravenously. His mother smiles at him and pushes the food around with her fork. When the boy is finished, she passes her mostly-untouched plate to him. Robert settles down against the side of a storage unit and spreads his sport coat over his legs, a makeshift blanket. He watches the woman wipe off the plates with wet-naps. He watches her spread blankets over the boy and kiss his head.

OUTSIDE THE GATES of the self-storage facility, the men in riot gear wait. A signal will come, and they will descend.

ROBERT DREAMS that he is in a desert, walking for miles, directionless. Each of the grains of sand in his dream is a tiny person. Thousands of tiny people shriek out in terror whenever he takes a step. He feels an overwhelming sense of pity, but tells himself that he's in the desert, and in the desert one must worry first of all about one's own survival. At night it's possible to freeze to death in the desert, he tells himself. I have to keep walking.

THEN EVERYTHING IS LIGHT and noise, and Robert is awake, his heart beating wildly, the dream, even the fact of having been asleep, forgotten. Floodlights surround the periphery of the storage complex. Orange doors pulled up, fought with, thrown open, guinea-piggers stumbling, running, masses of people being pushed forward by other masses, pressing into masses pressing the opposite direction, guinea-piggers falling and being trampled under the feet of other guinea-piggers. And from all sides, increasingly pushing their way in, men in black suits and riot gear, batons held at six and nine, shouting in a single voice MOVE MOVE MOVE MOVE, two-handed thrusting the batons forward in unison with each MOVE. The woman who looks remarkably like Viola is screaming out that she has lost her son, and in the next moment Robert has lost track of her in the mob. The feel of so many foreign bodies pressed against his, the stink of it—Robert wants to yell out that he is not part of this, he is something different than this mass, but there is an elbow against his throat, there is a hand on his face, fingers reaching for something to grip find their way into his mouth, into his nose, he presses his eyes shut in fear of having them mindlessly gouged out. It is impossible to say how many people he is in the middle of, it could be a hundred or a thousand, the world seems filled with them and Robert's options, suddenly, limited to the terrified mind of this press of bodies.

Now the men in riot gear have broken ranks and are falling upon them. When Robert chances to look he can see the great arcs of baton above the heads of the mob. Somehow even above the screams Robert can make out the dry crack of wood against a skull. They are being funneled in a certain direction—those who do not move correctly, or who get too close to the outside of the mass, are beaten, and thus the men in riot gear are training this new, corporate body, that they, with their helmets and floodlights, have called into being. Where to? Robert tries to push himself up on the shoulders of the bodies that press against him, and, just before being forced back down by other bodies likewise trying to push their way up, he catches sight of bodies being shoved into black, windowless vans. Going back is impossible; pushing to the side only presses Robert closer to the swinging batons; the mouths of the vans seem inevitable, and Robert can feel himself along with so many others pushing toward what he cannot avoid.

MEN IN ORDERLY UNIFORMS unload Robert and his fellow captives from the back of the van and lead them to a long hallway filled with other bodies sitting in folding chairs. Robert and the others are told to take chairs and wait. From time to time men in orderly uniforms come to lead one of the bodies to the doorway at the end of the hall.

ROBERT IS TAKEN by several orderlies to see a doctor, for processing. There are forms for Robert to fill out. "This is an observation period," the doctor says. "You should understand that we have a legal right to detain you for a seventy-two hour observation period, to see if you represent a threat to yourself or others." He sits on one side of a shabby desk, in a shabby office. He looks tired. Robert is one in a long line of bodies that the doctor is processing today. The doctor shuffles through some papers. Robert occupies a chair on the other side of the desk. To Robert's left and his right stand large men in orderly uniforms.

There's clearly some misunderstanding, Robert thinks. I have a JD, for Godssake. I am wearing a suit. But Robert's white shirt is dirty, torn in places. He's missing his suit jacket. He has been sweating, and pressed against other sweating bodies. "Why do I need to sign the forms if you already have the right to detain me?" Robert says, trying to grasp at whatever he can.

The doctor sighs and looks up at the ceiling. The orderly to Robert's left holds Robert's left arm behind his back and twists it, firmly but without undue violence, until it feels as though it might wrench free from its socket. Robert screams. The orderly to Robert's right hands him a pen.

"Here," the doctor says, indicating the appropriate line on the form. "Thank you. Here, as well, please," the doctor says. "Initial here."

"This isn't legally binding," Robert says. "I was under duress."

The doctor flips through his forms until he comes to one that affirms the patient has signed all forms free of duress, and the orderly twists Robert's arm behind his back until he signs it.

ROBERT CALLS VIOLA, from the depths of the hospital psych ward. “Viola,” he says to her voice mail, “Viola, pick up. For God’s sake please pick up. I’m at a hospital. I’m not hurt. They’ve taken us here. I was . . . there were all of these people, who participate in drug testing for money, and the police—or somebody—descended upon them. Upon us. They might have been working for Obadiah Birch. There is a man, he’s trying to organize the guinea-piggers . . . and there’s rumors of someone else, a man in fake fur and black goggles . . . but that doesn’t make sense. This sounds crazy. Of course this sounds crazy. There is no way, right now, for me not to sound crazy. Is that why you’re not picking up? Is that why you haven’t called back? But you haven’t even listened to this yet, of course. How could you? I just . . . I really would like to hear your voice right now. They, they have all of the people from the guinea-pig camp here, they picked us all up and are holding us for a 'three-day observation period' . . . except that, I've just learned, they found out about my insurance, that my insurance will cover a longer stay, they say that I need someone who can accept 'responsibility on my behalf' to come sign, to get me out. This is all illegal, of course, it's completely illegal. I've *told* them its illegal. They've told me . . . something about an obsession with the legality of things. Monomania. They can make anything fit. They've got a certain form, and they can make anything fit into it. Oh, God, I want to hear your voice right now. Please pick up. I don't . . . I don't know what number to tell you to call, if you get this message. There's a number on the phone, here, but it's been blacked out, and they've taken my cell phone from me. Someone else has taken my cell phone from me. Not the doctors. These kids, at the guinea-pig camp, a group of kids. Of course you're not going to pick up. None of this makes any sense. Why would you pick up? You haven't even listened to this yet . . . "

Robert calls again, crestfallen. Crestfallen, Robert listens to Viola's voicemail message. Robert calls again, and listens to the voicemail message again. If no one came to stop him, he could do this all day.

DOES IT MEAN SOMETHING that he's here, Robert thinks. Is it a kind of penance?

His roommate at the psych ward steals his shoes whenever Robert takes them off and goes shuffling down the hallway with them in his hands. Robert stops taking off his shoes when he sleeps. One night he wakes up to find his roommate carefully working his left shoe free from its foot. "Fine," Robert says. "You want the shoes?" He pulls off his loafers and throws one and then the other at his roommate. "Have them! By all means! Enjoy!" His roommate crouches in a corner of the room and cries. Robert lies down, waiting for the orderlies to come, thinking, Shut up, just shut up.

IT IS NOT A PENANCE. There is only one event happening after another, until Robert arrived here.

ROBERT IS IN a small room. In front of him is a bright white light. A man is sitting somewhere in front of the bright white light, facing Robert. Between them is a table. "Why does my head hurt?" Robert asks.

"Because I hit you over the head with the butt of my pistol. You were being uncooperative."

"I was asleep."

"You were being uncooperative in your sleep."

"Why do my ribs and arm and abdomen and chest hurt?"

"Because once I started hitting you it was difficult to stop."

"Are you a doctor?"

"I am an agent of the secret law."

"Could you turn off that light, for Christssakes?"

"No."

"Could you turn it down, at least?"

"No. The bright white light has important symbolic connotations: Truth, Justice, Righteousness, Grace, Purity. All of these things are important in our work, the work of the FBI, which is the preservation of National Stability. Is there anything I could get you that would make you more comfortable? A coffee, perhaps? A drink of water? No?"

Robert shakes his head. Robert's head feels like it's stuffed overfull with steel wool.

"I understand that at first the white light can be disorienting, uncomfortable perhaps, perhaps painful—but in time subjects get used to it. Often, they come to love it. We've recorded cases of subjects weeping when we take the light away. May I read you a testimony?"

"I suppose so."

"*I came to understand, after several weeks, that the white light was the all-encompassing mercy of God Himself, and I, poor sinner, can imagine nothing more joyous than the expectation, as I near the end of my life, of that white light's return*... This from a subject we interrogated in Algeria. I thought he was particularly eloquent, as regards the white light."

"What is that high-pitched squeal?"

"That's a high-pitched squeal. It has nothing to do with the white light. Here, Robert, let me show you some pictures."

"I can't see anything with that light in my eyes."

"You have to hold them at the right angle. There. See? Yes? Clearer, in the white light, than they could ever be by the light of day?"

"These are pictures of me."

"Of course they're pictures of you."

"At the guinea-pigger camp."

"Do you know that we have been investigating a series of shootings? Researchers, shot dead in Indianapolis, all of whom worked for the pharmaceutical industry? Who are you giving that file folder to, Robert?"

Robert sits for a moment in the glare of the white light. "You can't possibly think I was involved in the shootings."

"Of course we could think you were involved. It would take almost no effort on our part to think you were involved. You were present at the self-storage facility. You have demonstrated guinea-pigger sympathies, as evidenced by these photos of you acting sympathetic towards several guinea-piggers. You had access to records indicating which researchers were engaged in the most harmful and negligent drug trials."

"But I didn't have anything to do with it."

"I know you didn't have anything to do with it, Robert. Did I say you had anything to do with it?"

"Thank God," says Robert.

"I was only pointing out a certain fact. That fact being, if one were to choose to do so, one could easily make it *appear* that you had something to do with it. And as far as hard evidence is concerned? Photographs can be modified, film edited, fingerprints, DNA, ballistics, all can be tweaked."

"I feel like you're threatening me."

"Would you like something to drink? We have whiskey and vodka and gin and spiced rum and baijiu. For mixers we have orange juice and cranberry juice and several kinds of soda."

"I don't want a drink."

"I was only trying to be polite. You keep holding your head."

"My head hurts. Could you turn off that damn light?"

"There are people in the world who believe in such things as conspiracies, Robert." The man leans forward, arms crossed and resting his elbows on the table. "I don't. I don't imagine that you do, either. You are a practical man. But let us consider, for a moment, why someone less practical might believe in conspiracies. We tend to think of such people as paranoid, of living in fear of something that doesn't exist. And this might well be true, as far as it goes. But have you considered how comforting a conspiracy is? Instead of fearing the entire world and its capriciousness, such a man has a focus—which, moreover, serves to explain all of the otherwise inexplicable things happening around him. Are you religious at all, Robert? Never mind. I only bring it up because . . . Imagine, please, a roomful of believers. They are silent, waiting for the Holy Spirit to come and fill one of them, to cause that person to rise and begin speaking. Now let's say you're in that room, and I rise, and I begin to speak. You might ask yourself, how do I know that this person has actually been filled with the Holy Spirit, and isn't, instead, just some attention-seeker? You might say to yourself, I've been sitting here, quiet, not speaking, because I have been honestly and steadfastly waiting to be filled with the Holy Spirit, and here's this guy, standing up and talking about the same shit he'd be talking about anyway, Holy Spirit or no. You might, in other words, question my motives, question the purity of my intent.

"This would be the wrong question, Robert." The man places a new stack of photographs on the table in front of Robert. "It is entirely possible that I have base motives. But my motives are my concern, not yours. You are sitting in relation to something much larger than yourself."

Robert hold a photo up to the light. "This is my wife."

"Of course it's your wife."

"Why do you have pictures of my wife?"

"I have other pictures of your wife," the man says. "I have video of your wife. I have audio recordings of your wife, what her breath sounds like when she's coming, not with you, with another man. Would you like to hear that? Would you like to hear what your wife sounds like, when she's coming with another man?"

"Why do you have pictures of my wife?"

"Do you imagine that she sounds different, when she's with another man? So much of who we are depends on who we are with." The room fills suddenly with the sound of Viola breathing.

"Why are you doing this?" Robert begs. The breathing that surrounds him grows louder.

"We are doing this out of love," the man says, and places a baggie of pills on the table.

Robert stares at the pills, with a sort of horror. "I don't believe you," he says, finally.

"There were moments when she loved me," the man says. "Even if she did not love me all the time, there were moments when she did. I have photographic evidence of this. Video stills of her eyes, magnified to hundreds of times their original dimensions, in which one can see—scientifically, objectively—that she loved me, at least during that moment."

"I don't believe you."

"What? What don't you believe? That your wife's had an affair? You believed it enough to question her. Here: photographs! Of her eyes! Of her legs! Of her inner and outer thighs! Of the freckles underneath her navel! Of the soft skin on the underside of her arm! Of her left eyebrow, arched! Every part of her, photographically segmented and recombined right here on the table in front of you."

"I don't believe any of it. You're an FBI agent? You spend your time having affairs with people involved in your cases? You kidnap their husbands to ask about love?"

"Here's my badge—there!" the man says, pulling it from his neck and throwing it at Robert. "You want more photographs of your wife? You want video? You want transcripts of the call she placed to a women's health clinic? You want to hear the audio?"

"It's fake!" Robert yells, shaking the badge in the air. "All of it could be fake!"

The FBI agent throws photographs at Robert by the handful. Robert throws himself across the table and punches the FBI agent in the face. The FBI agent falls to the ground.

"Those photographs could be fake," Robert says, shaking. "You said so yourself, just a minute ago."

The FBI agent's nose appears to be broken. He pushes it one way and then the other on his face, trying to find the position it originally corresponded to. "Ow, fuck," he says. "Could you grab me that roll of paper towels over there? Ow."

"There is something in me," says the FBI agent, holding a wad of paper towel to his nose, "that rejoices even in this, suffering for your wife."

"She hasn't left me," Robert says, possibly to himself.

"Like this one time? We went grocery shopping? And every item she took from the shelves had its own, tragic charm. I've kept everything, everything. Except the milk and the apples. Those went bad."

"What is it about me that has stopped her from leaving?"

"She says that the two of you fell into marriage as if part of the set-up to a joke. The morning of your wedding day, she said, her dress somehow managed to rip from neck to ass. She had to borrow one of the bridesmaid's dresses for the ceremony. When she met you at the alter, she said, 'Well, Robert, which of us did you want?'"

“I’ve felt, since she lost the last child, like my life was closing in around me,” Robert says. “I haven’t been able to breathe, sometimes. I mean really. I try to take in a breath, and it stops halfway. I’ve lain awake at night, worried that I have emphysema. I don’t know any of the warning signs for emphysema. I mean, does it just happen? Just like that? One day you have it, and from that point on, life is a steady narrowing of the amount of air you can breathe in?”

The FBI agent sits on the floor, holding his head back to try to stop the bleeding. He takes out a pack of cigarettes and matches from his front pocket, manages one-handed to shimmy a cigarette out of his pack and into his mouth, and fumbles, trying to get a match lighted. “Do you mind?” he says. Robert kneels and lights the FBI agent’s cigarette. “Fuck,” the agent says. “I think I’m going to have to see a doctor about this.”

THAT NIGHT, Robert lolls in his hospital bed, cuffed to the bed's siderails. Suddenly, from all sides, comes a terrible rumbling. He has felt one earthquake in his life, and it wasn't nearly as jarring as this. He fights against the cuffs, trying to sit up straight. It feels for a moment as though the floor might give way. A stranger stands in his hospital room, a man in a fake fur coat and black goggles. Wordlessly, he uncuffs Robert's arms and motions for him to follow. Robert follows. Everything around him seems to be happening at a great distance. Scenes of horrifying violence, explosions, gunshots—the floor under Robert's feet shakes, it feels at moments as if the building itself might collapse. A nurse screams. An orderly stumbles blindly, collapses at Robert's feet. There are bodies everywhere. Yet it somehow never occurs to Robert to feel afraid, or even to wonder what is happening. Instead he simply follows—the fake fur coat makes its way through the violence, and Robert stays close behind.

The keypad that unlocks the elevator doors has been pulled free of the wall, and hangs by its jumble of wires—Robert stands beside the man in the fake fur coat and they ride the elevator down, past the first floor, the explosions he felt earlier rocking the entire elevator car, but neither Robert nor the man beside him showing any signs of distress; into the basement, where dust and flecks of paint rain down from the ceiling in time with the concussions that shake the floors above. Robert steps around bodies and follows the man into a tunnel, burrowed into the far wall, next to a row of vending machines.

They go down, down, down, into the darkness. It is impossible to say how far they travel. Finally their tunnel connects up with a series of others. This, Robert understands, is the guinea-pig underground: the ancient Indianapolis sewers that have expanded over the years, that have come to match the city itself in its sprawl . . . in the darkness there is the sound of movement, shuffling feet, indistinct orders barked out by men Robert can only just now make out, his eyes adjusting to the darkness: "Operation was a success, sir," in front of Robert is no longer the man he followed, but a guinea-pigger militiaman, dressed in camo with a black scarf obscuring the bottom half of his face. "We've taken the hospital. The Savvy Cavy requested that this one—" evidently Robert, "be spared."

The commanding officer sizes Robert up. "What's your name, comrade? Robert, huh? You look fancy, Robert, you used to be somebody? We're used to your kind . . . Fact of the matter is, plenty of our recruits have had some sort of substance abuse problem, even former lawyers. Were you a lawyer in your previous life, Robert? Were you on the other side? We've seen plenty of guys like you, has-beens who take up guinea-pigging to support a habit. Probably fucks the phase I tests up a teensy bit, having guys like you in the population . . . For the best, I say! Let them be fucked up! But once you're on our side, we need you clean. A requirement of the guinea-pigger militia, three months clean, minimum, we offer our own counseling programs if you need them, based on the RR rather than the AA model, given how hard it is to maintain a belief in any sort of benevolent higher power when you've got so much experience with earthly powers feeding you shit that makes your hands swell up to twice their size, your fingernails and teeth come loose, etcetera, etcetera . . . But sobriety is an absolute requirement! We're trying to fight a war, after all! And anyhow most of us come out of our latest phase I plenty out of our minds enough already, thanks!"

"Do you work with Jeremy?" Robert manages.

"Jeremy, that fuck," the commander says, already walking away. "Doesn't know his own ass from a prolapsed hole in the ground, pussyfooting between the courts and the mafia, trying to play one off against the other, and meanwhile Indianapolis growing darker for us each day . . . "

"Here, take this," a hand placing a pill in his.

"What is it?"

"It'll help with the fever."

Robert is laid out on a cot, shaking, muscles jerking, face contorted. A militiaman is assigned to his bedside. They've seen this before: discontinuation—he was on something other than just the tranquilizers they shot him up with at the hospital, and whatever it was, his body has grown dependent. Impossible to tell, without knowing the drug, whether the situation is life-threatening, but the symptoms look familiar to anyone who's come off certain long-term psychotropics: sweating, nausea, tremor, confusion, nightmares, "brain zaps." The only thing to be done, with the war going on aboveground, is to let him ride it out—

Beside his bed, a woman that could be Viola, or could be the woman he saw at the storage facility, the almost-Viola. She comes closer, until he can't quite make out her expression for the shadows across her face. She takes his hand, urges him wordlessly to his feet. They make their way out through the cell and further into the tunnels, past the ranks of training militiamen, who begin to grow larger and stranger the further into the tunnels they go, men clinging onto the walls and ceilings at impossible angles, men with the fur and general facial structures of rodents. Goggles turn into strange eyes, black and unreflective, set deep into the skull. Heads turn to peer at them as they pass, necks rotating a full 180 degrees, the intentions of the dull black eyes impossible to discern. Finally they are alone again in the blackness, and she is leading him to a light, set so far off in the distance that Robert is sure they will never reach it. "That flame has been burning here since these caverns were first explored, by the great-great ancestors of the guinea-piggers. It rises from the depths of the earth itself." Robert has no idea how long that is, but from the way she says it, he imagines that it's long indeed. He thinks of who or what was here before the guinea-piggers. He hears an unearthly sound from deeper in the tunnel, somewhere far beyond the fire. It is the sound of voices keening, the combined pitches alternating almost painfully between harmony and disharmony. And then somehow they are upon it, the fire, a snake tongue flicking through the mouth of the earth.

"This is a picture of our child," Viola or pseudo-Viola says. "And these are pictures of what might have been. Throw them in the fire."

The flame rises up to meet them. Viola grows more shadowy with each picture they throw in.

"And these are pictures of us," she says. "Do not look at them. Throw them in the fire."

"Oh God," Robert says. He is shaking now. "Everything?"

"We have hurt each other too badly, Robert. We have been judged by the secret courts. We have to go into the fire as well."

Robert throws one picture after another into the fire. It is hard. He is not throwing away what might have been but what was. Viola helps him. She holds him when he cries, with her hand she brushes the sides of his face, his hair. She insists, though, on feeding them into the fire. When Robert has trouble placing the next photograph into the flame, she guides his hand, gentle, unyielding.

By the end he has done it, he has fed every moment of their past into the fire. He falls back onto the cavern's uneven floor, her next to him. He is not even sure now of their names.

III

ROBERT WATCHES the riots on television from his parents' house in Geist, Indiana. Pictures of downtown Indianapolis look like a different place: windows smashed in, cars overturned, flames licking out from the faces of storefronts and businesses. Most of the city has been shut down, for three days. Now, though, on the news, they are announcing that the last of the rioters are being hunted down and arrested. Fire crews and police work around the clock to retain stability. Somehow, in the suburbs, things are quiet. Robert's mind is a complete and absolute blank. He imagines, that were he to peel his skin back, he would find nothing underneath.

HE VISITS his grandmother in the nursing home, and she starts screaming as soon as she sees him. A pit, a pit, he thinks.

VIOLA CALLS ROBERT to tell him that she is safe, that she is staying with some friends in the suburbs. "I'm glad to hear that," Robert says.

"Robert, where are you?" she asks.

"I'm safe," Robert says.

"I would think you would want to be together at a time like this," Robert's mother says.

"We're . . . separated," Robert says, searching for the word.

Viola calls Robert and when he won't say anything, she listens to his breath over the line. Robert goes to sleep each night in his childhood bed, feeling four times too large for his room.

THEN ONE NIGHT, sometime after the last of the riots, there's a tapping at his window. It's Viola, standing on one of the lawn chairs from the backyard. She makes a motion for him to pull the window up. Robert stares at her. She slumps, her forehead against the glass, looking more tired than Robert can ever remember her looking. He pulls up the window.

"You have lines around your eyes," Robert says. "I don't really remember seeing them before."

"Thanks," she says.

"No, I like them," he says.

"Are you going to come home?"

"Why didn't you answer your phone?"

"Oh God, Robert," Viola says. "If I had had any idea where you were—It must have been horrible—"

"I don't care what you were doing. I could live with that. But just—why didn't you answer?"

Viola thinks. She wants to answer this correctly. Not as in give the right answer, the one that Robert wants to hear, but to answer him as honestly as she is able. She says, "It wasn't that I didn't want to. It was—I didn't answer your first call, and I should have. Only it didn't seem like such a big deal, not to answer. And then it didn't seem to matter if I put it off, calling you back, at least for a little while. When I got the next call from you, I thought, I shouldn't answer this, I should call him back first. That is, I thought it would be better if I called you. But I was embarrassed about calling you, because you had just called me twice. Only slightly, but enough to cause me to put off calling you again. Then . . . I don't know. It added up. It became harder and harder to call. Putting it off made so little difference—that is, each decision to put it off seemed to make comparatively little difference in the overall situation. And the idea of finally calling you began to feel momentous. I couldn't even listen to your messages. I was afraid of what you would say.

"I finally listened to them a couple of nights ago. All of them, in a single sitting. Oh God, Robert. I'm so sorry. Robert, I'm so sorry." She attempts to hug Robert. Robert thinks, do I let her? Do I hug her back?

"Okay," he says, but does not hug her back. Viola pulls away from him.

"I don't want you to think I'm a terrible person," she says.

"I don't think you are a terrible person," Robert says.

Robert looks past her, at the window. After a moment he realizes, with no particular affect, that he is looking at his own reflection.

On Friday, Viola calls to tell Robert that her aunt has died.

ROBERT AND VIOLA drive through the husk of downtown Indianapolis. It looks, if anything, worse than it did on the news. They feel as though they are driving through an alien landscape. What could possibly live here, they think.

Their yard is littered with trash, their front door kicked in. Robert and Viola explore the house, half expecting to find someone sleeping in one of the rooms. There's damage, some missing items, but the house seems livable.

Robert sets to work repairing the door. Viola finds a broom, a dustpan. They work in silence, as if afraid that any unnecessary sound might break the truce, however brief, that has been called forth between them.

They sleep in different rooms, pass each other in the hallway like memories.

"WHEN MY MOTHER died," Viola tells Robert, "I didn't really even notice. Really, I didn't. For such a long time she hadn't been my mother, she'd been this woman who appeared every couple of months to tell me that she was getting better and that soon we'd be together again. By the time I was six, I was terrified of her. I was terrified that I would have to go live with her someday. But she never got better."

They are in Viola's old room in North Carolina and Viola is putting on her black dress. Robert sits on the end of her bed wearing his socks and his underwear and a white shirt and black tie. His suit pants and jacket are draped across his legs. "We were supposed to be there for each other," Robert says. "I could forgive you anything, except that."

Viola breathes in and out, carefully, and does not respond.

In the next room some distant cousins are trying to help Viola's uncle get dressed. Viola's uncle keeps calling out his wife's name, over and over, while the distant cousins grunt with the effort of trying to get his arms in his jacket.

"Her heart just gave out," Viola's uncle says, on the way to the funeral. "She was just a little thing, always had a fast heart. I used to say she was my hummingbird. She thought it was funny, me calling her that. The way she was always flitting from one place to another."

"How are you, Robert?" one of the distant cousins asks.

"Okay," Robert says. "I may be asked to resign from my firm. Not bad."

The funeral is in the chapel of the Hillsborough Street Baptist Church. "I didn't know Melissa that well," the minister admits. "But I have several trustworthy accounts of her character. She was loving and generous, more tidy than not, a woman of excellent mores and standards even if not a regular church-going woman per se . . . "

When it comes to be Viola's uncle's turn to speak, he says, "Missy and I never had any children. But I never knew a better mother than her in my life. Missy, damn you, what's Viola supposed to do for a mother now? You're just leaving her? You're just leaving me?"

ROBERT STAYS QUIET during a dinner with several of Viola's old friends. After dinner, as they're walking back to their rental car, Viola says, "You didn't have to come." When Robert doesn't answer, she says, "Look, I can find my own way back."

"That's ridiculous," Robert says.

"I don't want to be in a car with you right now," Viola says. "I don't want to share so little space."

"I came down here because that's what we do," Robert says. "We support each other. That is how this is supposed to work."

"This doesn't work," Viola says. "Jesus, Robert. None of this works."

They are standing near the edge of Moore Square Park, near the City Market. Just as Viola's starting to walk off, a man in a bomber jacket with a raw red face comes up to the two of them, waving like they were all old friends. "Hey. Hey I need to talk to you guys for a minute."

"Jesus," Viola says. "Not right now."

"You're the one who gave up," Robert says. "I never fucking gave up. You have no idea."

"No, listen: I need to *talk* to you," the man says, and shows them the pistol underneath his jacket.

"Jesus," Viola says.

"This all you've got on you?" the man says, looking through Robert's wallet. "What about her earrings? Give me her earrings." His eyes dart continuously from Robert to Viola, as if expecting one of them to tackle him. Cars drive by from time to time without stopping. Robert is trembling. He's ashamed and angry. He's thinking, Why isn't anyone stopping this? Can't they see what's going on? Viola hands over her earrings with a strange smile, as if she found the whole episode more awkward than terrifying.

The man tucks the earrings into his pocket, pushes the gun into the waistband of his pants, then takes off running through the park. Robert screams and runs after him.

"Robert," Viola yells. "What are you doing?" She's trying to follow after him, but not doing much of a job in it in her heels. She kicks the heels off, but that's even worse, because now she has to watch where she's putting her feet.

Robert keeps screaming. He doesn't think about what he will do if he catches the man. He doesn't think about the fact that the man he is chasing has a gun and he, Robert, does not. He doesn't think about what he would do were the man to turn and pull his gun. There's something furious and red in Robert's brain that blocks out the possibility of all other thought, so that all that is left in the world is a single thing made of running and screaming.

The man trips himself up on something or another and Robert's on top of him, catches him by the collar of his jacket and jerks him into the dirt. There's a wrenching sensation as Robert collapses on top of him. Then, hugely, the pistol goes off. Robert and the man look at each other, surprised, for a moment, as if neither had ever expected to hear such a sound, so close, in his life. The man studies Robert's face. Robert studies the man's face. Both Robert and the man are thinking: Which one of us was it? Robert feels himself for a wound. The man does the same. "The fuck," says the man. "The fuck." Both are unhurt.

Robert pushes the man's face to one side and scrambles on his belly for the gun, where it's fallen, a little over an arm's length away. Robert pushes himself to his feet and aims the gun. The man sits cross-legged in the dirt, looking up at him.

"I wasn't going to use it," he says. "Don't you see? What we've just been through is a miracle. You and me. You see what I mean? I've always wanted that, my whole life. I've always wanted to experience a miracle."

"Get on the ground," Robert says. "Face down. Into the dirt. Good. Now: my wallet. My wife's earrings."

"Here," the man says, flinging away the earrings and wallet. "Take it. Take your stuff. Don't you see what we've just been through?"

"Robert, what are you doing?" Viola says.

"Face into the dirt," Robert says to the man on the ground. "Give me your fucking wallet. Give it to me."

"Robert wait a minute, the police will be here—"

"I've got like three dollars on me," the man says.

"Give me your fucking three dollars then." Robert presses the barrel of the gun against the man's jaw. His entire body is trembling. The barrel of the gun, where it presses against the man's skin, moves as though trying to burrow itself inside.

"I'm reaching for my money," the man says. "Don't shoot me. Please for the love of God don't shoot me."

I want him to cry, Robert thinks. How do I make him cry.

The police show up and say "You two were very lucky. Normally we don't recommend that citizens attempt to apprehend an armed perpetrator. However, we cannot conceal our glowing respect when they do."

"The local news is coming by," one of the officers says. "Would you two like to be on television?"

"I think we ought to be on our way," Robert says.

"There are normally forms to fill out," the officer says. "But you know what? We'll take care of that."

"We recognize a kindred spirit," says his partner, clasping Robert by the shoulder.

"I DON'T KNOW what I'm going to do," Viola's uncle says. Viola is packing. Her flight is in a couple of hours.

"Are you going to keep the house?"

"Vivi, don't leave me here. I don't know what I'm going to do."

The distant cousins promise that they have space for Viola's uncle at their house in Zebulon, if need be. Viola's uncle and the distant cousins see her and Robert off at the airport. At the security check, her uncle hugs her close and says, just loud enough that she knows Robert can hear, "Vivi, when are you coming back home for good?"

The distant cousins try to comfort him. They assure Viola that he'll be alright. Viola keeps playing with the tag on her suitcase, nearly twisting it off. Her uncle doesn't smile or tell her anything's okay. Robert puts out his hand to shake and her uncle doesn't appear to notice. The distant cousins both give Robert hugs that go on a little too long.

The security personnel spend several minutes sorting through Viola's badly packed suitcases. "Ma'am, if you folded your clothes in an orderly fashion, and put all electronic devices near the top of your luggage, you wouldn't be holding up this line right now." Viola's uncle stands just outside the security checkpoint, longing after her like a ghost.

ROBERT DRIVES to the west side. Where the self-storage facility once was, is a pit, and a sign advertising new developments. Robert gets out of his car and hoists himself over the fencing into the pit. He looks out over a long stroke of nothing that has been cut into the earth.

Viola keeps expecting the FBI agent to reappear at the library, to call her, to materialize out of the shadows as she goes to unlock her car some night. It is like a long pause after a note, when you can't be certain another note will follow. Finally, she stops waiting.

ROBERT WANTS VIOLA more than he can remember wanting Viola. And yet he's so angry at her that he can hardly imagine having sex with her. When he sleeps next to her, he keeps turning towards her and grasping her tightly around the stomach, then turning away from her so that they're no longer touching. Eventually one of them gets up to sleep in the guest room. If it's Robert who's left alone in their bed, he masturbates, still smelling his wife on the sheets.

Viola thinks of what it means, that she wants someone to hurt her during sex. Does it mean that she's a bad person? Does the fact that Robert is unwilling to hurt her during sex mean that he is a fundamentally good person? Will he stay always by her side? Is he true? Is he chivalrous? Is he well-mannered? Well-heeled? Will he defend her against the evils that arrive time and time again in life? Or is he lacking in backbone? She thinks about when they were in North Carolina, when he chased and tackled the mugger. Was that backbone? Or was that an attempt to redirect other, overwhelming frustrations in his life, and hence (perhaps) a lack of backbone? Does she want backbone? Does it take any backbone to hit her during sex, when she so vocally wants to be hit? And what does any of this have to do with her upbringing?

It doesn't have a damn thing to do with her upbringing, she decides.

Robert holds Viola down on their bed. He slaps her. He doesn't feel anything. He slaps her again. She is breathing hard. He can feel how she pushes against him, he can tell—the word that occurs to him is "observe," he is observing—how much she is enjoying it. He thinks, I could continue to do this. He thinks, There's nothing actually difficult about this, about not caring. There's no particular reason I need to care. I could live my entire life in this space, empty, performing the actions that I need to perform at any given moment. Viola makes sounds like she is about to come and then she comes.

Viola sits on their back porch drinking a nonalcoholic drink she concocted from peach syrup and soymilk. She's wondering if such a drink already exists. If not, she'll have to give it a name.

Robert looks down on her from their bedroom window. What he wants, more than anything else in this moment, is for Viola to look up at him and smile. What is wrong with me, he thinks, that I can have, from moment to moment, such disparate wants?

Viola works in their garden in the back yard, pulling up weeds from between what she hopes will one day be fresh herbs. She has a book on fresh herbs that she's been following, hoping that this year her garden will come to something. How can she even be thinking about herbs, given everything that's been happening in her life over the past several months? And yet she still manages to pay some attention to her herb garden, from time to time. She sits back on her haunches and passes a moment, amazed at the fact that she can think about herbs.

Robert considers his future. Does he want to search for an associate position in some other law firm? Does he want to set up a sole proprietorship? Does he even want to stay in law? He thinks about other things he could do. He could manage a coffee shop. He could become a whitewater rafting instructor. He could teach classes on how to effectively prepare for the LSAT or the Bar exam. What is holding me in Indianapolis anyway, he thinks.

Robert goes to a bar on the west side by himself. He is sure that someone has followed him.

Viola lies in bed, eyes towards the darkened ceiling, asking herself, Is this the time he won't come back? Is this?

Driving home, Robert thinks, Can I even say the word love without swallowing my own tongue? I love, Robert thinks. That is a true statement. But what the hell does it mean? Can love exist without an object? Can love be a state of being, unfocused?

Viola thinks. Robert thinks. Viola thinks.

After a time, Robert crawls back into bed beside his wife.

He doesn't want to think that this is all love comes down to, that every night that he's able, he crawls back into bed beside his wife.

Viola thinks, Okay. Robert thinks, Is that all? Is it as cheap as that? I come back, she comes back, I come back? Viola thinks, Okay. That's something.

AND THEN THERE is a moment. Perhaps a week. Robert and Viola are happy. They go out to eat with friends. Viola works in the garden. Robert makes extravagant plans for their future. When they are together, they kiss. They have sex in the kitchen. Viola braces herself against the kitchen island and thinks that things are not so bad and, objectively, cannot get so bad. It is as if they are singing. Perhaps they are singing. Later, Robert makes lemonade from lemon juice and water and sugar substitute. They sit out on the porch and drink it and talk about how warm it's gotten.

ACKNOWLEDGMENTS

Selections from this novel, some in altered form, have previously appeared in *The Collagist*, *Atticus Review*, and *Red Lightbulbs*.

JAMES TADD ADCOX's work has appeared in *TriQuarterly*, *The Literary Review*, *PANK*, *Barrelhouse*, *Mid-American Review*, and *Another Chicago Magazine*, among other places. His first book, *The Map of the System of Human Knowledge*, a collection of linked stories, appeared in 2012 from Tiny Hardcore Press. He lives in Chicago.

LET GO AND GO ON AND ON

A NOVEL BY TIM KINSELLA

"I give Kinsella a five thousand star review for launching me deep into an alternate universe somewhere between fiction of the most intimate and biography of the most compelling."

—DEVENDRA BANHART

In *Let Go and Go On and On* the story of obscure actress Laurie Bird is told in a second-person narrative, blurring what little is known of her actual biography with her roles as a drifter in *Two Lane Blacktop*, a champion's wife in *Cockfighter*, and an aging rock star's girlfriend in *Annie Hall*. Kinsella explores our endless fascination with the Hollywood machine and the weirdness that is celebrity culture.

"ADCOX'S *DOES NOT LOVE* IS A BOOK I DIDN'T THINK WAS POSSIBLE: A PERFECT BALANCE OF RELATIONSHIP DRAMA, BITING SOCIAL SATIRE, AND NOIR THRILLER. THE STORY MOVES AT A QUICK CLIP, SKIPPING SEAMLESSLY FROM MOMENT TO MOMENT. NOT UNTIL THE LAST PAGE, DID I COME UP FOR AIR, LOOK BEHIND ME AND WONDER, 'HOW DID HE PULL THAT OFF?'"

—JAC JEMC, AUTHOR OF *A DIFFERENT BED EVERY NIGHT* AND *MY ONLY WIFE*

"LIKE THE INSTRUCTIONAL DVD ON ROUGH SEX WATCHED BY ITS MARRIED PROTAGONISTS, JAMES TADD ADCOX'S DOES NOT LOVE STARTS GENTLE, THEN BUILDS TO HIGHER INTENSITIES. A FUNNY-SAD STORY OF THE HEROISM OF RETAINING HUMAN EMOTIONS IN A SOCIETY QUICK TO PATHOLOGIZE THEM, THIS NOVEL LOOKS HARD AT THE POSSIBILITIES AND EMPTINESSES OF LOVE."

—KATHLEEN ROONEY, AUTHOR OF O, DEMOCRACY!

"LIKE OUR BEST CONTEMPORARY WRITERS, JAMES TADD ADCOX SEES THE PREVAILING GRAY OF THE AGE, THE MAPS DRAWN WITH FUZZY, EVAPORATING BORDERS, AND THE HILARITY THAT RESULTS FROM OUR INSTITUTIONALIZED